Training Sweet Jolie

Dirty Voyeurs Book 1

J. P. Newmon

J.P. Newmon

THIS BOOK CONTAINS REFERENCES to fraud, extreme sexual themes, cheating (not between main characters), stalking, and some violence. Please read with caution if you are sensitive to any of these issues.

I wrote this for fun, you should read it that way.

CONTENTS

Sir

I SEE YOU. I know you feel invisible and alone right now, Kitten, but I see you. Watching her soak in her bathtub has become a nightly ritual for me. The excessive mound of bubbles covers all my favorite parts, but patience is all it takes to get a show. Eventually, everything melts away, and the bounty is revealed. I take a sip of whiskey, swallowing slowly as I study her. She's *perfect*.

Chapter 1

Misery

Jolie

MISERY. THAT'S ALL I could feel. My bathtub had long gone cold, and the bubbles melted into nothing but a foamy coating on the surface of the water. Sweat from the once steamy water drips off the end of the faucet with sporadic little plinks into the cold tub. I stare numbly at the corner where the caulk between the tile and porcelain is peeling. I have all the supplies to fix that, but never the motivation.

The edges of the tub are like ice helping to spread the numbness over my body. The dripping sound from the loose drain echoes, misery. Fat tears roll down my face as I sob in silence into my lukewarm pinot grigio. I lean over the edge of the tub to turn up the volume on my laptop, Mazzy Star's "Rose Blood" pours from the speaker in a gritty tempo.

The stemless wine glass slips in my hand, and I almost drop the whole damn thing in the tub. I struggle to catch the glass. The sound of water sloshing and my ass slipping in the tub clashes with the sad ambiance I had created like a record scratch. I recover the glass and slide back down into the tub, turning the scalding hot water back on with my toe. It is the fifth time I've refilled the bathwater. Maybe I can boil the bad feelings away.

Ugly.

Worthless.

Unlovable.

The poison of dark thoughts consumes my mind. Why does this keep happening to me? This cannot be normal; functioning during the day and depressed at night. Misery. How do I deal with this? How can I cope? I'm wasting in this cycle; fear and anger knot my insides. Fear that I will never find happiness or contentment. Anger at what he did to me, leaving such deep scars on my heart.

The bottle clinks the side of the tub as I grab it by the neck and refill my glass with a messy slosh. The memories eat at my insides, and I need to numb this pain, even if the relief is short lived. He was so attentive, made me feel important and loved. All these years down the road though…. I see that he took deep seated fears and insecurities I had and exploited them to control me.

I finger the side of the wine glass as my thoughts sink into the past. Sometimes I think I could be freed if I tell someone. If I let out all the ugliness into the universe. I want someone to reassure me, yeah that sounds like the relationship from hell, you're not overreacting. Your feelings are real.

Prostitutes, ON OUR FUCKING HONEYMOON!!!!! —because I was "too innocent to satisfy his taste in the bedroom". Looking back at the photos I should have seen that he was detached from me. Bored. Disappointed. When I tried to talk to him, I was accused of making up stories and trying to play victim. Then finally came THE AFFAIR, the one that broke me. I had always had a funny feeling when he spoke about his female coworker.

I had no concrete reason to think ill of their friendship, just a gut intuition. He began staying late for work, he stopped calling home in the evenings. Instead, I got text messages telling me he would be out late and don't wait up. When it all came out, he walked out on me. Now I am on my own and I have all this self-hate to unlearn from the years of gaslighting and emotional manipulation.

I lay in the bath and dwell on the hurtful memories and sob into warm wine while I shiver in my cold tub water. My eyeliner pen seductively whispers my name from where it rests on the edge of the soap dish. Maybeline Tattoo Studio; it's my favorite because it doesn't come off in the water. When I'm ready to take it off I have to scrub my skin raw and that too is part of the satisfaction of self-loathing. I begin to write in jagged scrawl over my chest, stomach and arms.

Tonight, I adorn my face in degradation too. I write hurtful, hateful thoughts all over my skin. Somehow this relieves the tension in my chest. Like the truth sets me free. I write the sad truth of a sad girl over and over again to cope with my anguish. My nightly ritual of self-loathing over my lost dream of a 'happily ever after'. No little house, no accumulated years of happy memories, and no tacky Christmas ornaments documenting our life of love together for me.

I'm physically exhausted from hours of crying. Clunking my wine glass down on the edge of the tub, I knock the end of the laptop. It drops it into the water with me. FUCK! Waves of soapy bathwater wash over the side of the bathtub like a tsunami as I scramble to rescue the device. From the depths I pull the soaked laptop, the screen black and water pouring out of the keyboard. Guess that it is ruined now. I leave it on the bathroom floor. I don't even dry off; just flopped in the bed sopping wet from head to toe. BB, my golden retriever, huffs from her bed, a little scolding for disturbing her slumber. "Sorry BB, love you." She snorts in response and we both drift off to sleep.

The night sky is illuminated by the silvery shimmer of the moon. I see its reflection rippling in a puddle as I lean closely to lap up cool liquid. My gritty tongue coming out to clean my lips and then my paws. A cool breeze grazes through my fur and sends electricity up my spine. I feel alive and energized in the night. I feel free. The puddle begins to vibrate rhythmically distorting my reflection and then everything is gone.

Fuck you alarm clock and your mother's a cunt. I slam my hand down and beat that bitch to death before cursing at myself for staying up so late last night. I really need to pick a new sound for the alarm, I can't listen to Ripple anymore. Makes me want to stab myself in the ear. It takes me a few minutes to organize my thoughts and realize it is morning. The dream is a ghost at the edges of my mind. I scold myself for drinking all night in the tub and then only having the energy to do the bare minimum to get out the door.

I always feel like complete shit the next day. Why do I do this? I should drink more water, exercise, and sleep a full night. Maybe I wouldn't be so fucking sad if I had a healthier lifestyle, took some vitamins. Lofty ideals for sure, I need a keeper because I can't be trusted with my own wellbeing. Snuggling under a blanket on a day off with a good book and cup of coffee sounds so good right now. Maybe I'll do that tonight instead of being a pathetic "sad girl", yeah right.

I go through the route motions of getting ready for work. Sit on the toilet and pee while I put in my contact lenses, gross, I know, fuck off. Then I wash my face and brush my teeth. I jolt when I look in the mirror and see the scribbled words still covering my face, breast, and rib cage. Scrubbing aggressively with makeup remover until my skin is red and sore, I erase the ones that could be seen outside of my clothes. I'll leave the rest to carry me through the day. They'll give me strength. Oils and serum to make me beautiful.....probably a scam but I'm too nervous to skip it. I don't want 90-year-old me to curse my name for not even attempting skin care.

I sip my coffee while I apply eyeliner. Sleeptoken blares from my phone. I don't make too much fuss over myself, except the 20-minute detour where I try repeatedly and fail at cat-eye liner, damn. It looks so good on other women but always seems awkward on me. Lamenting, I look down at the purple lipstick on the countertop. I love the color. So vibrant. Makes me think of the person hidden inside me that I can't quite set free again. My hand hovers in front of my lips, the intention frozen in the mirror. The application of a color impossible to complete in the gray of my existence.

Gravel crushes under my tire as I pull into a parking space behind my shop. I own this little weird shop that is like a hybrid between a vintage record store and witchy mystic shop, Jolie's Eclectic &Vinyl. Not the most creative name I know, but I couldn't come up with anything that didn't sound cheesy or wasn't already taken. There was a time I would never have imagined myself running a small business. The idea of keeping up with invoices and inventory seemed daunting. I had a dream though. I wanted to make a place where old and new could mesh together and thrive.

Gary thought it was a dumb concept. He said there would be too much variety of merchandise in the store, and not having replenishable stock of my items wouldn't satisfy my customers long term. He thought they would get bored with what we had on the shelves and stop coming into the shop. He was wrong though. Our inventory is unique so the turnover of items on the shelves has kept the shop interesting.

We have tarot cards, crystals, vinyl records, essential oils, and pieces by local artists. We even have a little backyard area with an herb garden. My favorite part is the giant rosemary bush, it's so fragrant you can smell it from the back office when you open the window. I planted it as a living commemoration of the shop's opening. It's a pretty freakin' cool little shop if I say so myself. I love meeting all the talented artists and craftsmen in our community. Krista and I go "treasure hunting" for unique items and goods at local craft fairs, pawn shops, estate sales, and flea markets. Lately though I haven't had as much enthusiasm for searching out new stuff. Krista and I have made several plans to go out on "treasure hunts", but I keep breaking our plans: like yesterday evening.

She is already here, CRAP. I pick a sprig of rosemary from the bush before going inside, holding it to my face I breathe in its aromatic scent and try to exhale the remnants of negativity in my lungs. As I walk through the back door I'm immediately pinned with a disapproving look from my bestie and only employee. Ducking into the office, I try to look busy and avoid Krista just a little longer until I can get my big girl panties on. I'm pulling out invoices and firing up my computer when she barges through the door. I swear sometimes I think she is the owner and I work for her. We definitely need to work on some boundaries.

"Why do you let his ragged ass keep control on you?" she says. "You have already given him everything and he walked out. Threw it away! Why do you let him steal this time from you too?" Her electric pink wavy bob bounces emphatically along with her scolding. She is an edgy rocker girl with tattoos and pierced everything. Krista is a no-nonsense, ride or die. It's why I love her. But it is also biting me in the ass right now.

"I don't know what you're talking about Krista." I continue "working" to try to cut off the scolding, shuffling papers that don't need shuffling and stapling random shit together.

"So, are you going to look me in the eye and tell me you didn't lay in the bathtub all night, drinking and crying over that sorry SOB?"

Damn, how does she do that? She forges on, determined to drag me kicking and screaming out of my delusional misery. "You need to get laid. A lot. You need to get out there and date a bunch of random guys, one after the other. Get your feet wet talking to men you know you have zero interest in and have dirty, dirty sex. So, when you do find someone worth your time you can really enjoy the experience, feel confident, and quit packing Gary's shit around."

She sits down on the edge of the desk and puts her hand on mine to stop the erratic and aggressive stapling I'm doing. "I don't care that you broke our plans; I get it. I'm your friend and I understand your quirky ass. But as your friend, I know this doesn't stop with you missing a girls' night or blowing off coffee with me. You are letting his memory suck all the joy from every part of your life."

Emotion catches in my throat making it difficult to respond. I listen to my very intuitive friend express her concern, knowing I have the evidence of its validity written under my shirt. Still, I deny the truth. "No, Krista, I'm not. I just have all these hard feelings I need to work through before I can fully move on. I'm not trying to bring my emotional baggage into the next phase of my life."

She sighs and gives me the look. The classic 'I'm going to let you be for a while, but this conversation isn't over' look. She's not wrong though. I know it and she knows it. I really am giving him all my power. He is continuing his life and loving every minute, and I am miserable. How do I break this cycle though?

I tried getting an online therapist. One of those situations where you message back and forth. The advice I got was a mix of drinking more water, exercising, and try to remember the good times he and I had. I decided cathartic crying in a bubble bath was better than spending hundreds of dollars on that bullshit advice. I really do need to drink more water though, so maybe they were onto something with that one. In fact, I should go refill my tumbler right now but instead I'm going to have my fifth cup of coffee and it's not even noon. I lean back in my office chair and take a deep breath, inhaling the scent of rosemary from the back garden.

After lunch, Krista and I straighten shelves and rearrange displays. I like to keep the shop organized throughout the day so there is less work at closing. Krista is changing the arrangement of hand thrown mugs to be more visually aesthetic. I'm dusting bottles of essential oils and organizing crystals that have gotten mixed around when she clears her throat. I look over in her direction.

A man has walked into the shop and is browsing next to the counter. Krista jerks her head a few times in his direction. Hell no! I raise my eyebrows and flatten my lips to show her I'm not biting. Cold and calculated determination crosses her face. She turns and heads to the back storage room where we keep the 'to be inventoried' stock. As she passes the man she sweetly says, "If you need any help, the shop owner is right over there" and gestures in my direction.

All I can do is smile and nod. I want to murder her. I could hide her body under the rosemary bush. She disappears through the back door. Nervous sweat is pearling on my forehead and down my back. I make my way to the counter and pretend to organize something underneath.

There's a vintage mirror in a box back here. It's a heavy brass cast metal mirror on a stand. The mirror was busted out of the center, but the frame is so beautiful and ornate I couldn't leave it behind at the estate sale. It would make an excellent statement piece on an entry way table even if you didn't replace the mirror. It just needs some polishing to really show its beauty. I place it on the counter and take a polishing rag to the frame, desperate to look busy. I adjust the angle on it to get between the intricate design with my cloth. When I look through the center, I see the customer looking down at me with an amused smirk. "Oh, there's no mirror in there. I was confused for a moment, I thought 'damn I'm looking good'." I just blink back at him. I think there was supposed to be a compliment in that statement, but it also could mean he thinks I look like a man.

I must have taken too long to respond because now his smile is gone, replaced with a scowl, and he is shifting awkwardly on his feet. "So, you uh, you own this little shop?"

"Yes."

"Okay, I'm Scott. I just took over the hunting and sporting goods store up the street. I've been meaning to come in here and... take a look around." He leans his elbow on the countertop bringing his face closer to mine. His breath smells like garlic.

"Okay."

"Okkkkaaayyy. Uh, real nice place. You seem to have a little of everything." He shifts so that both elbows are on the countertop now and he is leaning even closer to me.

"Yes, we do."

You know that saying about watching an accident happen. How everything seems to slow down but you still can't intervene. That's how I feel in this conversation. I know I'm failing. I know I should say more, elaborate. Bat my eyes. But I can't seem to change anything I'm doing. I can only stand here with my resting bitch face and short answers, watching myself make an absolute mess out of this simple conversation with the opposite sex.

I recognize this guy. I've passed him several times on the street going and coming from our respective shops. He's attractive, I guess. He looks like he would own a lumber business or ranch in one of those feel-good Hallmark romance movies. Average height, blonde hair, smooth face. He's even wearing a tan Carhartt vest over a flannel shirt. Seems like he should be hot though considering it's early summer.

He looks so out of place standing in my shop. We get hipsters and witchy girls. Crunchy moms. College kids rebelling against mainstream manufactures. We don't get woodsy outdoorsmen looking for rose quartz jewelry and rosemary oil. If he came in here just to talk to me, then I bet he is filled with regret right about now.

"So, you got someone to watch the shop for a minute? We could grab a cup of coffee."

"Oh no, I've already had like 5 cups today I really shouldn't drink anymore."

I did it again. Shut him down without actually meaning to. I mean, I'm not interested but I wouldn't mind getting coffee with him. He seems like he could be nice. He looks okay. But I am ruining this opportunity because I have no idea how to talk to people, especially men.

"Oh, okay. Well maybe another time then. Nice little shop you got here, Jolie. See you around." Annoyance filled his tone as he said his goodbyes.

"Yeah, thank you for stopping in. See you around."

The shop door chimes as he leaves. Krista is standing in the doorway of the backroom with her arms folded over her chest and mouth hanging open. "What the hell was that?" Her face contorted with shock.

I sigh and roll my eyes. "Krista, that was me... being me. You know when you say I should just relax and be myself when I talk to men? Well, that's it. Tada!!!" I wave around some jazz hands for emphasis. She walks toward the counter and inspects the vintage mirror I had set out. "You need some practice. Why don't you try one of those dating sites? You can just practice talking to the opposite sex without the stress of being in person. You're always saying you express yourself better when you are writing. Isn't that why you did messaging with that online therapist instead of going to someone in person?" Krista is right. I get so stressed out by talking to people in person. It takes months for me to feel comfortable and relaxed around people.

"Yea, but you know how that worked out. And anyway, aren't those sites all cringy? You don't really know who you are talking to. People can put anything up there, even fake pictures."

Krista begins wiping down the counter. Rubbing away fingerprints from the glass. "Jolie, that goes both ways. Just get some practice talking to someone who isn't your shitty ex-husband. I'm not saying find your next husband on there."

"I'll think about it okay?"

"Okay."

Chapter 2
SwtJolie

Jolie

After work, I take my laptop to the electronics store on the other side of town, the repair man said it was a lost cause. Maybe he could have salvaged it if I had immediately put it in a container of rice to help dry it out (probably would have thought of that if I hadn't got drunk and sad until well after midnight). I momentarily grieve the loss of photos and documents I'll never retrieve.

Some stuff might be saved on my external hard drive, but I can't remember the last time I backed anything up. Honestly, I don't use this laptop for much more than a stereo these days, which is why it was in the bathroom in the first place. However, I do need to have one for a backup in case anything happens to the office computer at work. The electronics repair man, whose name is also Gary (* eye roll* no wonder he can't fix my laptop, Garys are useless), recommends I check the pawn shop downtown if I need a cheap replacement. Gag, I hate downtown, it's so sketchy.

Gross, I need a shower just looking at the store front of this pawn shop, Frank's Steals N' Deals. Steals is right I bet. I'm probably gonna end up with some criminal's old laptop and then they'll come after me and I'll end up on a true crime podcast. I pull my sleeve over my hand as I grip the door handle and let myself inside. The aisles are made of seven foot metal shelves full of the other people's goods. It's almost like a grimy version of my own store. The difference being that people who sold their belongings here probably thought they'd eventually get them back. I pass a section of jewelry. I wonder if any of these are from scorned women, maybe I should have brought my old wedding rings with me. Gary could at least help me get a discount on my new laptop.

At the far wall I see a counter with a little service bell. Reaching out with my sleeve still covering my hand, I give it a little tap. The sound jarring in the otherwise silent shop. A greasy man appears behind the counter (assumably Frank) and smiles at me with a mouth full of rotten and capped teeth. Fuck. "Welcome to Frank's Steals N' Deals, what can I do ya for sweetheart?" I hate that saying. It makes me feel like I'm being solicited with innuendo. I try to smile without being too encouraging. "Hey, I was wondering if you have any laptops for sale?"

"Well, little lady, I'm sure we can find something for ya." Frank grins and licks his bottom teeth, the four in the front all rotted and black. Great, I bet I'm about to get a real "deal". He heads to a room behind the counter and returns with a large box. He pulls out a series of laptops that look like they got dropped-kicked out of an airplane. He gives a sly grin as he tells me, "I got these here for real cheap but don't know if any of 'em work too good. You know, all sales here are final so if you take it home and it don't work, can't come back and complain to me." I smile and nod. None of them look like they work.

"You don't have anything else?" I ask hopefully. His expression turns enthusiastic, he claps his meaty hands together and then reaches under the counter to pull out a shiny new laptop. Of course, the first ones are the terrible decoy options to convince you to purchase this more expensive one. He is so proud of himself. Buddy, I just want to buy one and get the F out of this store, we could have skipped the song and dance. He places it on the countertop with a flourish of his hands as if he is presenting a diamond tiara. "Well, I do have this one. It's gonna cost you a little bit more but it's pretty new."

"Great, how much?"

"Oh, I couldn't let it go for less than $1K."

"That's the price of a brand new one," I say flatly.

"I tell ya what, you look like a sweet kid", he is staring right at my chest now and I cross my arms in front of me to try and deter him, "So, I'll make ya a deal. I'll give it to ya for $600 and I'll throw in the power cord for free." What the fuck dude, the power cord wasn't gonna come with it?

"Okay, plug it in and show me it turns on and that the mouse works, then you have a deal."

"You're the boss, little lady." He smiles at me, clearly enjoying the haggle. I turn on the laptop, check the mouse, and open a few internet browsing screens until I'm satisfied it isn't a total lemon. I wiggle the power cord to make sure the attachment isn't shorted. "Okay, I'll take it," I say, closing the laptop and unplugging the power cord. "$600 even, right?" He leans forward on the counter, his eyes roving over me. "Yeah $600 even, unless you got something to trade? I could be persuaded to bring down the price a little." He waggles his eyebrows at me for emphasis. Gross, like I would do a quicky in the backroom for him to take $50 bucks off the price? "$600 sounds great to me." I slap my purse on the counter for emphasis that I'm super-duper not interested. As I walk out of the shop he calls after me, "You come back sometime ya hear."

I put the laptop on the floorboard of the front passenger seat. Once I plop my ass in the driver's seat and lock the car doors, I let out a big exhale. That was a disgusting exchange in there. How many women does he fuck in the back room to be asking me so casually? And further, if nasty-teeth, greasy-haired Frank can get laid so easily what the fuck am I doing with my life? I bet Frank doesn't go home and lay in his bathtub crying over lost love. Honestly, it doesn't look like he lays in the bathtub at all. I put my car in gear and pull away from the curb. I need to get my life together.

From the pawn shop I swing by the local grocery store to pick up some quick items. They should give me my own designated parking space considering I'm here almost every evening. Maybe I should start buying my wine in bulk. No, that would be fully admitting I've hit rock bottom. I throw a spare jacket over the laptop on the floorboard and head inside. It always smells like wet carboard in here and I'm pretty sure they mop the floor with a mixture of super glue and motor oil. How can linoleum be sticky and slippery at the same time?

Roaming the aisles with the basket in the crook of my elbow, I pretend I'm just browsing and not here for a singular purpose. Toilet paper, bubble bath, some baby carrots (they are just going to die in my fridge, I should have gotten the blueberries instead) and some other random things I hope distract from the fact that I'm really in here buying another bottle of pinot grigio. Oh, I should get some electronics cleaning wipes. Need to make sure Frank's funk is cleaned off the new laptop. I shutter at the thought of what nasty germs might be all over his hands. I get a mental image of him fucking someone right on that countertop and I throw up a little in my mouth.

It's been the same checkout boy every day for the last week. I can just imagine what he is thinking when he rings me up. 'This sad lady again, always in here buying wine.' Honestly the only thing that could make this worse is if I was also buying tampons or maybe cat food. I could be a lonely cat lady. That idea might just have merit. BB would probably be pissed. I've always loved cats, but Gary was "allergic". I questioned if that were true. I would go to the pet store and hold kittens just to get a cuddle fix and then come home and hug him, no reaction. That fucking dickhead.

Maybe I'll get 50 cats now that I live on my own. When I drunkenly slip in my bubble bath and die, they can eat my body. I'm jolted from my dramatically anticlimactic demise daydream by the annoyed greeting of the checkout boy. I step up to the register and set my items out on the belt. I add a pack of gum, some hair pins, toilet spray, ChapStick, and a Slim-jim to my pile as I smile and move up the line. I've probably added $50 of nonsense to disguise my $10 bottle of white wine. Maybe the store manager will offer me a deal like Frank did. Sling a little cat for a monthly supply of pinot?

I feel a tall presence step up behind just a little too close. Great, someone behind me in line is also judging my purchases. I just need to be really still and look straight ahead and maybe they won't try to make small talk. A hand comes down on the candy rack behind me, it rattles under his perch. I turn around slightly and see Scott. "Well, hey there Jolie baby. I didn't think I'd run into you twice today. You planning a relaxing evening at home?" He nods toward the wine and bubble bath on the belt. Uh, now he is probably picturing me naked in a tub full of bubbles. I don't know what is worse, that he might be thinking that or the sad alternative truth of my nightly ritual. He looks me up and down with a sleezy grin. Scott seems way more forward now than he did earlier today and I'm not sure what to make of that. Maybe the difference in seeing me in a casual setting verses my place of business is bringing out more of his true nature.

"Oh yeah. I'm a home body." I wave my hand over the length of my haul on the counter. "Just going to watch some TV and relax tonight." I turn back toward the register. At least at the shop I could fiddle with something to hide my nervousness. I step up closer to the register to pay.

"Anyone to cuddle with while you do all that? Shame such a pretty woman would have to be all alone."

Now that was bold. I don't want to encourage him; I just want to get out of this store and get home. Plus, he is kinda giving me the ick right now. "Nope, just having a peaceful night on my own." Even if I admit I need to have more of a social life, Netflix and chill is not on the menu tonight. He continues to crowd me at the register as I take the receipt from the checkout boy.

"Let me know when I can take you out for coffee. I'd really like to get to know you better, Jolie."

Okay, maybe he is just trying to be friendly, and I am just a social dumpster fire. I smile and nod at him as I take my bags and get the hell out of this store. My heart is racing as I get back to my car. Maybe I should feel lucky that the offer of coffee is still on the table with my multiple failures at social appropriateness. I always let Gary control the conversation and make the decisions. Where we were going, what we were doing that weekend. He dominated all our conversations and if I tried to interject any thoughts, he cut me off and talked over me. I was fine fading into the background. Now I can't seem to break free. Krista is right, I need to work on my social skills, or I will for sure be buying crates of cat food with my wine in the very near future.

I go home and walk BB, do some chores, eat random shit from my pantry and refrigerator that I hope isn't expired. I should really buy proper groceries, but it's hard to be motivated when I live alone. I could cook BB gourmet meals; she would appreciate that. I pat her on the head and pay the cheese tax. We sit on the couch for a little while and watch internet videos of yoga routines, BB's head resting in my lap while I lazily pet her.

I should be doing it along with them but instead I'm just watching and making bogus plans to start this up as a hobby. Maybe BB and I could learn together. The ticking of the clock slowly overwhelms my thoughts. When it gets really quiet and dark is when I struggle. The wine is chilled and waiting for me in the refrigerator. I start my bath water and dump in half the bottle of bubble bath, another reason I have to go to the store every night. They should make bubble bath stronger. If you aren't at risk of suffocating under the bubbles, then are you even taking a bubble bath?

I balance the laptop on the toilet seat instead of the edge of the tub. This should be a safe distance away to prevent a repeat of last night. When I got home, I placed it on charge so it should have enough battery to last me a few hours just playing music. This weekend I'll work on saving frequent websites and passwords. For now, I login to my music streaming service and pull up Lana Del Rey radio. It's the mood for tonight. Tears dribble down my cheeks. I feel pathetic. I'm wasting my life. Leaning my head back against the wall I shudder out a long exhale. What the fuck am I doing?

After my bath, I take the laptop over to my bed and start searching different dating websites. These all give me the ick. I search internet reviews of each one. Some of them seem like they are only sites for catfishing. There are a few that look like potential options. I start to create an account just so I can feel it out. Now I just need a login name. Something cute, but not too cute. I need to seem interesting. Some mystery even. Nothing too identifying though. I'm not trying to meet these people in person. I select an age one year younger than I am and a neighboring state. Now I need a username......

Babygirl37...... no that's no good.

LnlySwtHrt..... not that either.

SwtJolie...... that has a good ring to it, but I don't want to use my name.

Damn, this is harder than it should be. It doesn't matter what the name is, I just need to put something down so I can get started.

CurvyBabe..... okay, eh, maybe I like SwtJolie better. No one can hack you with just a first name, right. Just do this already, Jolie. As soon as I hit the button to confirm creating the account, the laptop shuts down. The entire screen goes black. I hit random keys, try the power button, nothing. I'm sure the battery was still at 25% life; it shouldn't have just turned off. Fuck I knew that asshole, Frank, cheated me with his "All sales are final" bullshit! I sit the laptop on my dresser and flop myself down on the mattress like a toddler having a tantrum. Surely there is some law that protects purchases even if they are from a pawn shop, would love to look it up on the internet, oh wait I can't cause the fucking laptop doesn't work. I turn out the light with a huff and try to go to sleep.

The next morning, I get ready for work, throw BB her tennis ball a few times in the backyard, and then head back to the bedroom to collect my lemon of a laptop. When I approach the dresser, I stop in shock. The laptop is on. It's working. Shit. I whirl the mouse around and open the internet browser to check it out. Everything works. Maybe I should let it sit on the charger while I'm at work. I close it up and pack it and the cord in my computer bag. I'll plug it in in the office at the shop. I'm afraid to leave it plugged in and unattended at home. This thing might blow up.

I pull into the parking lot a groggy mess. I need gallons of caffeine to get thought today. At least my job is peaceful. I get to be surrounded by beautiful and healing things that bring people happiness. It's been an excellent morning. We've had a steady flow of customers and sales. I'm standing at the counter putting invoices into our system during a lull when Krista brings up dating sites again. "You don't have to go on actual dates you know. You can just use the messaging feature. I can help you choose a picture and set up your profile if you want?"

"Okay, okay Krista. I did look into a few options last night and researched the reviews. I started to make an account but then my new laptop fritzed out. I'll try again tonight. Satisfied?"

She sits back and eyes me like she doesn't believe me at first, but she relents. "Keep me posted, okay?"

"Okay."

It's late at night; I lay in bed and give myself a pep talk. Kitchen clean, walked BB, laundry put away, I vacuumed, mopped, dusted baseboards, shopped online...I have procrastinated on this for as long as I can this evening. I have tried to talk myself both into and out of finishing setting up an account. Maybe it was providence last night when the laptop shut off at the last minute...No, Krista is right. I need to take a step somewhere. I do want to date again, I'm just not sure where to start.

My mother would stroke out if she knew I was talking to strangers online. Loneliness was drowning me though and there was no way I was ready to start dating in real life. I have no confidence or true feelings of self-worth. Yeah, all that feminist mindset is great in theory. Girl Power, Fuck the Patriarchy, I'm entering my villain era. I could get down and feel invigorated by all those things in theory, but not in practice. Not yet. I look in the mirror and can't help but feel used up; past my prime. Who would really want this too curvy, anxiety riddled, cries to herself in the bathtub every night washup? This is nothing serious, I tell myself. This is for practice. This is getting my toe in the water, so I don't feel like a complete idiot on real dates. This is a beta test to see if there is a market of interest in women like me from men who aren't complete creepers.

I researched the internet for the safest websites last night. My search history should pull up the ones I looked at already, so I don't need to start from scratch. There's a website I don't recognize at the top of the list but its link is purple so I must have searched it last night. I don't remember it though, "Good Finds". Hhmmm, I click the hyperlink and still don't recognize this page. The website recognizes me though, and I'm automatically logged in? I have a partial profile set up too?

There is a picture of me from one of my social media accounts and some basic demographics on me. I don't remember setting this up, this wasn't the website I was on last night when the laptop shut down. There's already a message waiting in the inbox. I back out of the website and search reviews for "Good Finds", and they are stellar. Pictures of happy couples giving firsthand experiences and the highest rating for internet safety. I guess I did make a profile???

I click back into the site to look over the information on my account. The "about me" section is filled in with basic stuff like year of birth, city and state. There's generic shit like loves long walks, dogs, reading, and coffee. The profile picture is from a Halloween party last year, I'm dressed as a black cat. Krista took that picture. In fact, she forced me to go. I remember how good I felt all dressed up, confident. Not like my typically lost self. I had fun and I needed to get out of the house. I hover over the inbox tab and see a message from someone named FirmD_m40. I don't open it yet. Instead, I search the site for possible matches.

There are several profiles recommended to me. I'm not sure how this site decides who would be a good match. These guys are all pretty diverse. There's a lumberjack, a biker, some guy in an expensive suit, a gym bro...it's like a lineup of all the romance novels on my e-reader. I see another message pop up in my inbox. JustinJ_84 and he is online.

Holy shit, this is really happening; I get up from the bed and pace the room a few rounds. I spy the kitten ears from that Halloween party hanging on a necklace rack on my dresser. I snatch them up and put them on, a little extra confidence never hurt anyone.

JustinJ_84: Hi, hru?

I click on his profile. He looks normal. Kinda average looks, plain t-shirt and jeans.

SwtJolie: I'm good, hru?

*JustinJ_84: *Smile*....I am good too.*

SwtJolie: Great, got big weekend plans?

JustinJ_84: Not much. Just chilling. What are you here for?

That's interesting. I didn't realize people got on these sites for normal conversations too. I just assumed everyone was horny and looking to hook up.

SwtJolie: I guess I'm not sure? I'm new to this.

JustinJ_84: Lol....no worries. Married?

SwtJolie: Divorced. You see many married people on here?

JustinJ_84: No, but I always ask upfront just in case. I'm single too. How's dating been going?

SwtJolie: Haven't really started yet, just getting my feet wet here, I guess.

JustinJ_84: Yeah it can be brutal out there.

This is a good way to blow off some steam without all the hoops to jump through, you know.

SwtJolie: Yeah, I'm sure it is.

JustinJ_84: So, you horny?

.... well, I guess we are just going to jump right in. How do I respond? I guess just "yes" or "no". I'm honestly not horny, I'm terrified. This is so out of my comfort zone. That was the point though, to practice talking to men in a controlled space. I can just click out of the screen if I want to end this conversation, and I'll never "see" this person again. They can't stalk my phone or show up at my work. A small, wild and rebellious part of me that has been locked away whispers in my ear, "just go with it". And why not? I read spicy romance all the time. Surely, I can just draw from those scenes to have a sexy conversation. I can just have fun. This isn't supposed to be serious, right?

*SwtJolie: Oh yeah, I totally am. *wink**

*JustinJ_84: Uh, lol okay...*smiles*.*

Uh, I'm such a loser. Okay girl, channel some of your favorite authors. You can do this. Think sexy thoughts.

JustinJ_84: What are your tits like?

Gulp. Okay, what would one of my favorite romance authors say? I look down at my boobs, never really thought they were that great. I don't want to lie about my body. One of the main reasons to try chatting was to increase my confidence in my looks. To show myself that even though my body wasn't Insta-worthy it was still desirable.

SwtJolie: I'm a D cup; with sorta teardrop shape, large dark nipples.

JustinJ_84: I'd love to have my hands on them right now. I bet they bounce and jiggle when you ride cock.

Okay, guess I didn't fuck that up. He seems pleased. The feminist in the back room of my mind is giving me the stank eye for putting value in a man's opinion. She'll just have to take a seat for now. We can talk about this later.

SwtJolie: Yes, they do.

JustinJ_84: Squeeze them for me baby. Massage them and pinch your nipples.

SwtJolie: Okay....

At first I consider just moving along the conversation but then I decide what the hell, I rip my top off and squeeze my breasts rhythmically.

JustinJ_84: Are you clean down there or fur pie?

I'm kicking myself for not realizing I would be describing my body in graphic detail. Of course, he wants to know what all I got on the other side of this screen. Especially if I'm not sending pictures or videos, nope. So that leaves me with a "tell all" about my body so this guy can imagine all the nasty things he wants to do until he cums on his hand.

SwtJolie: Clean. Totally smooth.

JustinJ_84: Nice. I'm very oral. Love to eat a clean pussy.

*Lay back for me baby..... *licks ur mound*.*

Hold ur lips open for me so I can get a good view.

SwtJolie: Okay.....

I'm not really sure what to say to that. If this were real life, I would just be following the directions he gave. I feel like I need to offer more to the conversation than just a series of "okay's". I do as he asked though.

*SwtJolie: *reaches down and opens lips for you**

JustinJ_84: Mmmmmm, damn baby you look so good.

I'm starving. Going to eat you up.

licks up and down ur slit

sucks ur clit

I bet you taste and smell so good baby.

I know full well that this is a fake compliment. He is just imagining this. Maybe he's never licked a pussy in his life, but damn if I don't feel emboldened by his praise. Shit, what does that say about me if I'm so affected by compliments from a stranger on the internet.

SwtJolie: Oh, that feels so good.

JustinJ_84: Are you getting wet baby?

I reach down and to my surprise, I am wet. And my clit is getting sensitive. All this just from his brief description of licking my pussy. But if I think about it, if I picture this is a real encounter...damn does it sound good. It's like an interactive spicy scene from one of my romance books.

SwtJolie: Yes, I'm wet. I'm spreading it around my pussy for you.

JustinJ_84: Mmmmm.

runs tongue all over

licks ur inner thigh and bites

Keep rubbing yourself for me baby.

I'm stroking my cock while we talk. I'm getting so hard.

SwtJolie: That sounds so good. I bet it would feel good too.

*JustinJ_84: *rubs cock over ur clit**

Do you like to suck cock baby?

*SwtJolie: If it's good cock. *smile**

JustinJ_84: Ha, open up for me baby. Put your fingers in your mouth and imagine it's me. Keep rubbing your clit with your other hand.

*SwtJolie: *opens mouth**

JustinJ_84: Mmmm ur mouth is so warm and wet.

Swallow me baby, gag for me.

SwtJolie: I swallow up and down your shaft. Ur precum tastes so good.

Hold my head and thrust into my mouth.

JustinJ_84: Aaaahhhhh, yes baby.

U feel so good I'm not going to last long.

U going to swallow for me?

I rub my clit and dip into myself while I think about his dirty words. While I imagine his hands in my hair and his cock filling up my mouth. I spread my wetness all around my clit and apply firm pressure. This feels so dirty, so wrong, but so good.

SwtJolie: Yes, every drop. Give it to me.

JustinJ_84: Ask properly

eyeroll Of course he said that. What is it with men wanting women to beg. Then I consider my favorite books. The ones I loved the most had really great plot, but they were all dark romance. Filled with dirty degradation and male dominance. So, maybe I liked the begging too.

SwtJolie: Please fuck my mouth and give me your cum.

JustinJ_84: That's a good girl.

That little phrase right there. That is what I want to hear. A lightbulb turned on in my brain. It's not like I walk around my life wishing someone would call me a good girl. You don't know how good that feels until it's actually said to you. I imagine him leaning close to my ear, his voice deep and gritty. The whisper of his breath floating across my skin, sending shivers down my spine. His cock ungodly far down my throat, pushed in as he leans down to speak to me without losing his place. I think about fingers gripping my hair at the base of my scalp and the sting in my eyes at the pain. I shudder and I cum, right here on my bed. Soaking my sheets with my laptop laying at my feet while I play all this dirty talk through my mind.

JustinJ_84: AAAHHHHHH!!! Yes baby, I'm filling up ur throat. Drink it all baby. Clean up my cock.

I'm still coming down from my own climax. I'm not sure how to gather my thoughts right now. So, all I say is......

SwtJolie: Yes, Sir.

There is a lag in response. I'm not sure if I've said the wrong thing, did I lose his interests right at the end? Just as I'm really gearing up to overthink this, his reply comes through.

JustinJ_84: Go get cleaned up now. You should go to bed, it's late.

SwtJolie: Yes. Goodbye.

JustinJ_84: Bye.

And just like that, the conversation was over, and he was gone. I'm not sure what to think of myself. I just had dirty online sex with a stranger. Check that one off my bucket list. Maybe it's a little cringy but why was that so hot? I get turned on when I read my romance books. How is this so different? Other than it being a two-way conversation and not me alone with a book and a vibrator. Part of me feels used by his quick departure. But I shouldn't.

He was clear about his intentions for the conversation. A conversation that I consented to and participated in. No strings, no fluff, just two people who needed a release with a mutual understanding of the score. I shouldn't feel guilty about that. In fact, I don't. I feel good. I didn't worry about my weight, my boobs, my ass, or my cellulite. And the high of being told "good girl"... I rub my pussy slowly while I relive that in my mind. That was good. Real good. I could almost climax again rethinking the conversation.

Maybe "Justin" is a short king with a 1" wiener who lives in his mom's basement and plays online shooter games all day. Maybe he isn't 39 years old, maybe he is 75. I try not to fall down the rabbit hole of possibilities. I hover the mouse over the inbox then suddenly, the laptop shuts off again. Fucker! Does this thing have a timer set?! I quickly shower to get cleaned up, change into a fresh nightgown, and tuck myself into bed. I have an early day at the shop tomorrow. Tossing around in my sheets I can't seem to get the experience out of my head. Sleep evades me. I flip over on my stomach and hug my pillow to my chest.

Irked by how aroused I was by such little show of affection and the fact that I'm still completely turned on, I grind my hips into the mattress, seeking just a little pressure, rocking slowly, moving my hips forward and back while squeezing my thighs ever so often. I spread my thighs wide and arch my back then bring my legs back together, pressing my face in the pillow in frustration.

The norms of conventional society bring up feelings of guilt mixed into the excitement of this new venture into self-gratification. I have never really felt at home in conventional society though. Even my shop rest on the fringe with its crystals and homeopathic goods. Letting go of deep rooted obligations to be boring, to be a quiet girl who doesn't make waves, to let my own passions be smothered for the benefit of others desires is a difficult thing to do. What do I really want? I want someone who will take control, treat me with reverent degradation, and make me succumb to the dirty desires of the flesh. Hanging on to the fantasy of being called "Good Girl" while being sullied by cum all over my face has my arousal soaring.

I roll to my side. My thighs are slick again; I run my finger down over my pussy then in between. Bringing my knee forward, opening my thighs I delve deeper into myself. Slow thrusting deeply into myself then pulling back to run my index and middle finger on either side of my clit. I fall into the fantasy of a dominating man's hot tongue tracing the pulse of my neck and then grunting dirty words into my ear, "Are you going to be a good girl for me? Open your legs and let me see you work that wet hot pussy."

I roll onto my stomach and spread my thighs wide, pulling my knees in and riding my fingers while grinding into the heel of my own palm. I imagine a dark stranger sitting at the foot of my bed enjoying the show. Cheering me on, "That's my dirty girl, ride your pretty fingers until they're soaked in cum." The fantasy changes to me riding his face, grinding my clit on his nose and lips, his hands gripping my ass cheeks so hard they'll bruise.

I cry out into the empty bedroom as I cum, rutting against my own hand. Panting and legs shaking I come down from the high of climax, finally feeling relieved and sleepy. I pull myself up and take a whore bath in the tub just to clean my pussy up before going back to bed. I don't even take off the nightgown. I just squat in the tub and gather handfuls of water from the faucet to rinse the soap and cum away. I throw myself back on the mattress with a thud, closing my eyes and drifting away.

Chapter 3
Here Kitty Kitty

Come on, turn the computer back on. I tap the index finger of my left hand impatiently on my mouse. I've been tracking this Peterman douche for months now and I'm losing patience. I was so close to finding his location from pinging his laptop, then he shut it down and hasn't had any activity since. I need those encrypted files he has hidden in there so I can wrap up this client's case. When Congressman Robert's wife hired me to dig up all kinds of dirt on her husband in retaliation for the laughable divorce package he offered her, I thought this would be a quick-and-done job. This is my expertise after all. Finding out people's dirty details.

I run a blackmailing firm, under the radar of course, hacking into computer systems, bank accounts, social media...expunged documents no one thought they'd see again. Scorned lovers, ex-business partners, hopeful business partners, politicians... they all come to me for information. Nothing is secret or sacred. It can always be found, for a price. And people are willing to pay top dollar because I am the best at getting the information they want without a trace of how it was obtained. I can fake the legal acquisition of it if needed.

Everything about my business is underground, off the grid. You can't even find me on your own. I find you. I started hacking for fun as a teenager, I soon learned enough to get the attention of some high up "businessmen". I did favors in exchange for favors until I had enough owed to me to start my own information exchange empire.

I couldn't have been more wrong about this being a quick gig though. I thought what I got on his infidelity was damning enough, but his wife is going for blood. He could have paid her off by giving her continued access to a life of luxury, but now she's set on bankrupting him and hopefully sending him to prison for embezzlement. How does that saying go, "Hell hath no fury like that of a woman scorned"?

Phase one: was hacking all his devices to obtain incriminating photos and files. Everything I uncover for a client I backup on my servers just in case I need to retain access for any reason. Photos and a separate personal calendar for all his meet ups were easy to copy. Then came catching him in the act of his cheating. I posed as a potential hook up to catfish him on what he thought was an anonymous chat site. I had the unsuspecting congressman thinking he was connecting with a hot piece of ass. Little did he know, I was documenting everything he said, all the dirty pillow talk and promises of a good time.

He's been stepping out on the misses to play submissive to male dominates. It didn't take long for him to hit me up with a greeting this time. I learned from past attempts that he never responded when I greeted him first; I'm sure this is out of a false since of safety on his part but it's unbecoming of a real submissive. Tsk, tsk. Very rude to ignore your "Sir", very rude indeed.

The username I created this time was catnip for him. A few "You wanna be a good boy for me" lines and listing out punishments I thought he needed was all it took to get him interested enough to give me the good stuff. He preferred that website because he thought nothing was stored when he logged out; the site itself does not, but I do. Screenshots are forever my friend. A warning people should heed; always assume the person on the other side of the screen is up to nefarious schemes.

I personally don't care what a person consents to behind closed doors, but his conservative constituents sure will. His political career is effectively over based on this offense alone. I don't think his wife really cared about his unconventional sex life; she had her own side relationship to keep her occupied. No, this is about power. About making him feel as humiliated as she felt by his attempt to basically discard her in the gutter after she had endured all those years by his side. I got the damning evidence I needed complete with some sad photos of his – I can't even call that a penis – he eagerly shared with me. At the end of it, I wanted to scrub my eyeballs out with whiskey.

Phase two: was hacking all his accounts and compiling evidence of his financial crimes. I think we have enough to take down the congressman but wifey isn't satisfied yet. If she's willing to pay for all my efforts, why not. Hacking his accounts is what led me on this goose chase of tracking down his scumbag partner, Jonah Peterman. I'm just about to call it quits for a while when I get a ping that the laptop has been turned on and is connecting to a public wifi signal. I get to work finding a location, Fayetteville, AR.

I hack into the laptop camera expecting to see Peterman's fugly face but instead I see an angel. She is staring intently at the screen, inspecting the laptop. Her dark hair and eyes glistening in the electronic glow. Full lips, the bottom currently being dug into by her top teeth, molding it into a plump morsel begging for my attention. The dip of her bountiful cleavage in her low-cut shirt perfectly in view by the way she leans toward the screen. I get into the microphone and am greeted by the sweetest voice followed by a slimy male's. They're haggling over the price of the laptop.

That makes sense. Peterman must have stashed the device in a pawn shop while he regrouped. The laptop powers down and the sight of my angel is lost. Fuck! I didn't hear if she committed to buying the laptop. I'll have to wait and see if she uses it again. I get to work finding the location of the pawn shop, but by the time I get myself into its security camera feed, she's already gone. I go from frame to frame checking all the views, no angel in sight.

I don't leave my post at my desk all evening, waiting. Pouring another finger of whiskey, I pass the time researching this little city. It has a good variety of shopping and outdoor activity. Not far from secluded foothills. A cabin out there would be a perfect escape from the stresses of life. I've always wanted to eventually move out of the city into the quiet of nature. I get sidetracked looking at real estate in the mountains when I get an alert that the laptop has turned back on. Switching my screen over, I can hardly keep my excitement in tow. There is my angel again. I immediately switch my screen over for a full view through the camera. I want to be as close as I can possibly get to this ethereal being.

Looks like she is standing at a counter. Her dark hair falling over her shoulder. Her eyes look a little red, her mascara is smeared. Has she been crying? I mirror the screen so I can see exactly what she is doing. Her cursor swirls around the screen as she opens a music application and selects an artist playlist. The sad selection pairs perfectly with her sad expression. She takes a sip of wine and then turns her back to me, disappearing from my view. I hear the roar of a faucet turning on full blast. When she returns, I'm blessed with the view of her naked chest.

Her large breasts sway with her steps. A dark, tight nipple comes right up to the camera as she lifts the laptop and carries it somewhere. I could almost reach out and catch it with my teeth. She sets the laptop down giving me a view of a porcelain bathtub with bubbles cresting the edge. Her gorgeous ass comes to view as she steps into the suds. Oooh, must have gotten the water too hot sweetheart. She sinks in slowly with a scrunched-up expression on her face. The tight grimace of her lips is soon replaced with a perfect "o" as she reclines in the tub, the bubbles coming up to hide those beautiful breasts from me.

I watch, enraptured as she lounges in the bubbles. She sips her wine and pats at the bubbly mountain peeks on her thighs. Her expression of sadness deepens; tears roll down her full cheeks. She doesn't make a sound. She doesn't try to wipe them away. We are trapped together in this moment of reverent sadness. Like a spectator appreciating a fine work of art in a museum, I take in every detail of her. Trying to find clues within the artwork to explain the meaning. After the bubbles have all melted, she goes to rise from the tub. Foamy rivers run down her belly, over her smooth pussy, and between her thighs smearing the writing she's applied to her skin. I'm eye level with that delicious center of hers as she steps over the side of the tub. I ache to reach through this camera to touch her pussy and lap the drips of water from her skin.

She wraps a thin dusty pink robe around her wet body and ties the belt. The wet material quickly turns see-through as it soaks up the water from her flesh, her dark nipples shining bright. We go on a little trip as she carries the laptop to her bed. I'm starting to see a trend in her color choices, romantic hues of emerald, wine, and rose. Her robe slips down giving me a little more access to those wonderful breasts. Her wet hair dripping water down her collar bone and then trickling down the center of her chest.

I'd be licking that clean if I were there right now. On my mirrored screen I see what the brat has gotten up to. She's searching dating websites. Over my dead body. I watch as she researches several before settling on one to start up a profile. I'm tempted to stall out the website but then I have a better idea. She'll give me information I can use to find her. Just as she finishes up and goes to click submit, I shut the whole laptop down. It's late, my little pet needs to go to sleep.

The username she chose. SwtJolie. Mmmm, the name immediately conjures thoughts of a sweet and obedient little pet, eager to please Sir. I don't even know if she is a submissive, but I see a flash in my mind's eye of a dark-haired voluptuous woman adored with ears, tail, and collar. My cock hardens at the image. A warmth spreads in my chest. If she was looking through dating sites, I assume that means she is looking for a relationship. Look no further, my pet. I won't allow her to go on hundreds of dates with other men. Good thing I have a special set of skills to fix this problem.

I use the information I obtained from her creating a profile to do some digging into her life. It doesn't take long to find her social media and other public record information. Cute how she tried to throw me off with subtle lies about her city and age. I see she was divorced not long ago. Gary looks like a real winner. Good girl getting away from him. Images on Google Earth give me a view of her home. She lives on a quiet little street. The neighborhood looks like something out of a feel-good family movie. Nice sidewalks, shade trees, every house with a front porch and well-kept lawn. They aren't giant homes, humble but loved. Her little shop looks interesting too. Jolie's Eclectic and Vinyl. The website shows a few pictures of the inside and the smiling faces of my pet and a coworker.

After a few hours of research, I turn the laptop back on and watch her sleep. Lucky me because she kept it open and facing her bed. Morning comes and I get little glimpses of her as she walks past the screen and view of the inside of her shop when she took us to work. She's been pulling up frequently accessed websites and saving login information. Her bank account, social media accounts, shopping websites…. I peruse them leisurely, learning more and more about her habits and her preferences. When she isn't actively using the laptop, I spend my time searching for the hidden files. It's hard to believe Peterman has the computer skills to hide them this well. Finally, I find what I'm looking for, but it will take some time to fully copy and unencrypt them. While I wait, I pull up an adult supply website and go shopping for my pet.

Presumptuous of me to assume she is a pet player, I know. I haven't even confirmed if she is a submissive or even in the market for a Dom. My gut tells me she will make the sweetest little kitty though. There is something about her expression in that photograph I found from the Halloween party. The demure tilt of her chin and pouty expression, with mischief simmering just beneath, gives me great expectations.

I scroll through pet gear imagining what each would look like on her. She's too sweet for leather, something furry, with bows and rhinestones would suit her much better. Ear and tail combinations come in all colors, reds, pinks, calico, and black. Yes, black ears. Like in her picture. I add a black tail with a white tuft at the end to my shopping cart. Hmmm, maybe some accessories too. A collar, a leash, some fun things to wear... I'm interrupted by the completion of the file downloading. I'll have to check on my pet later.

After backing up the files on my server, I open them on my tablet and take it with me down the hallway to the gym. I need some activity after sitting at my desk for so many hours. I scan my thumb print to unlock the door then make my way over to the treadmill. Placing the tablet on the tray of the treadmill, I hit the program keys and put in my earbuds. Multitasking while I work out, I turn on the audio function so my program will read the files to me while I run. Two hours in the gym and one hot shower later, I've finished reviewing the data. I'm ready to compile a report to my client, but that can wait until tomorrow. It seems the congressman has been a very bad boy. This is enough to send Roberts and Peterman to prison for fraud; I get the feeling there is a third accomplice somewhere in the mix, but I can't figure out who just yet.

It's early evening and my pet should be home from work by now. The pounding of my feet echo in the stairwell as I jog up the flights leading to the ground floor and exit the building. My office base isn't large: a conference room, three private offices, and a gym with aerobic equipment, weights, and a sauna. Having a smaller operation makes it easier to stay under the radar. Being located in the basement of an "abandoned" warehouse gives an added level of anonymity. From the street it looks like a rundown building with boarded windows. Underneath is a fully remodeled secure home base with private access. I obtained ownership of the warehouse above to keep the city from demolishing it.

Crisp night air fills my lungs. Anticipation of the opportunity tonight brings has electricity coursing through my body. I walk three blocks to the private parking garage where I park every day. Can't have fancy cars sitting in front of a rundown warehouse all the time; that would for sure scream drug deal to the local police. I climb into my Mercedez and fire up the engine. One of the reasons I love this car is the massage feature in the seats. It hits the spot after a long day leaning over a desk. I set up the tablet so I can enjoy my favorite show while I drive home to my apartment, Kitten TV.

Her after work routine gives me more insight into her personality, the real her, and I'm falling hard for it. Her sweet interactions with the dog, BB, are endearing. They romp through the house like best friends. She completes her chores while dancing to 90's music. My pet really has some moves. Her ass jiggles around while she works her spray mop like a stripper pole. I can't help but grin. I should have made popcorn for this show.

I make my way up the private elevator and into my apartment, almost taking out the entry way table with my hip because I can't tear my eyes away from watching her. Moving on muscle memory around my kitchen I pull out one of my prepped meals from the freezer and throw it in the oven. While my dinner heats, I switch from the tablet to my TV, synching my feed to her so I have a better view on the big screen. By the time my dinner is ready, and I settle on my couch, it's on my favorite part of Kitten TV, bathtime.

Tonight's bath doesn't disappoint. She washes and massages her breasts with the loofa, and I can feel my cock harden with anticipation of talking to her later if she goes back to the dating website. My pretty girl likes to linger in the bubbles, soaking and pondering her life. I lean closer to the screen trying to will her with my mind to get out of the tub and back on the website. Then I have an idea. Picking up my wireless keyboard, I give it a few strokes and I interrupt her music streaming. The prolonged buffering encourages her to get out of the tub and move on with her evening.

We're sitting together on her bed. I enjoy the way her silky peach nightgown sticks to her nipples while she searches the internet for where she left off the other night. She finds my website and takes a few minutes to work through her confusion that she already has a profile set up. I hope she likes the picture I chose. My perfect little kitten. After finding it on her social media, I can't see her any other way. My choice is validated when she finds those same ears and puts them on while she explores the website. I'm rapt with anticipation as she hovers her mouse over the message I left her but that quickly turns to frustration when she doesn't click on it, instead she searches the other options of men. Ultimately it won't matter who she chooses but the reflexive jealousy still hits like a brick; I never thought I'd be jealous of myself.

She takes her time looking through them all. I wonder if she can tell they are all the same man. Every picture is me with various hair styles, facial hair combinations, and different clothes photo edited into backgrounds aligning with interest and supposed locations. There is me chopping wood, on a motorcycle, fishing, woodworking. She slowly inspects all the profiles that are "matched" to her. I can hardly stand the waiting. I finally message her from one of them, impatient to get her attention. If left to my timid kitten this could drag on all night. I need to talk to her.

Justin_84. The profile shows me hiking. I added a dog to up the relatability. We go through a few hellos and what brings you here. Her nipples showing through the damp robe are teasing me and I need to see more. I turn the conversation to sex, I don't want to build too much connection. I don't want her to like Justin, I want her to like me. And I want to see how my kitten follows direction and what she's willing to show me. I see she's honest with her personal descriptions. Good girl. And even though this is only an online chat (as far as she knows) my pet is following along with all my requests. She lays back and I get a perfect view of her smooth pussy. The way she spreads herself open for me is almost like she knows I'm watching. Her savoring her own fingers as if it was a giant cock in her mouth has me groaning in delight. And the "Yes Sir" at the end is icing on the cake.

After saying our goodbyes, she continues rubbing her pussy while moving the mouse over to the inbox button. Sorry kitten, you'll have to wait until tomorrow to talk to someone else. I shut down the computer so she can't continue to indulge herself. Keeping the keyboard inactive and the screen dark I'm able to keep watching as she gets ready for bed. Poor baby, tossing and turning.

She throws the covers back in frustration revealing her delicious silhouette. She rocks her hips into the mattress; my greedy girl didn't get her fill earlier. I wonder, when was the last time she had a good satisfying fucking?

Precum weeps from my erection as she begins riding her hand. I reach into my sweatpants and pull out my throbbing cock. My fingers rippling over the swollen veins as I squeeze and stroke myself to her performance. Already primed from our earlier encounter I'm ready to explode as she cries out. Will you chase pleasure with such raw fervent when we are together Kitten? Or will I have to draw you out, teaching you how to leave your inhibitions behind? I pour myself out onto my bare chest wishing it was hers I was cumming all over.

Chapter 4
Hello Sir

Jolie

FUCK YOU ALARM CLOCK and your mother's a cunt. I reach out and bask around on the mattress for my phone to shut off the blaring. I stretch my muscles and try to rouse myself for the day. Reaching my arms out toward the pillows and arching my back with my butt toward the ceiling, it feels so good to stretch and hold this position. I rub my face into the mattress and grunt. Trudging into the kitchen I start the coffee pot, set it to gigantic ounces and place my black cat Halloween mug under the drip. After it finishes, I fill it to the brim with creamer, using my electric whisk to froth it up. Some splashes over the edge and I lick up the side of the cup to catch the drip...mmm the creamy dreamy goodness. I really think I could lick up a cup of just the cream by itself.

BB gets her breakfast and a few tennis ball fetches before I head out to work, ready to face the day. Interestingly, I feel a little lighter than normal, a little happier and more rested. Just like last time, the laptop is working again this morning. I take it to work and charge it again. Every so often I try out something like adding a password to a saved website just to keep it active. Maybe it has a timer or something, like when your phone reminds you it's bedtime. I make a mental note to check the settings later.

I'm sitting at my desk in the office humming to myself as I work. Krista saunters in and plops down in the plush dusty rose accent chair. She fingers the fake fiddle leaf fig plant. "When are you gonna dust this plant, Jolie?" She swipes her finger across the broad leaf and holds it up for me to see how disgusting it is. Scooting my desk chair back, I reach into the bottom drawer and pull out a handheld disposable duster. Still humming I walk over to wear she is sitting and begin to mindlessly dust the leaves.

She crosses her arms over her chest and eyes me suspiciously for a few seconds then asks, "Is that Bejeweled? Are you humming Taylor Swift? Girl, what did you get up to last night?!" She walks over to the desk and sniffs my coffee mug, I roll my eyes because I know she's checking for liquor. "Nothing, I just read a little and went to bed early." I finish dusting the plant and move onto the floating shelves on the back wall. It has been a while since I even thought about cleaning these, gross.

"Mmhhmm I bet, you didn't do any online chatting?" She follows me to the shelves and leans in close to whisper over my shoulder, "No sexting with strangers?"

How the fuck does she do that? I need to check my house for surveillance. I swear she has the place bugged and wired for cam-eras. I side eye her as hard as I can, "Maybe", I shrug. Customers start trickling in to browse the shop, so I'm saved for the moment. Krista walks back toward to the office doorway then stops and looks over her shoulder at me: "When we close for lunch, we are walking down to Dripping and you are spilling your guts young lady." With a flourish she turns back and heads out into the shop.

Fuck, how embarrassing is it going to be to tell her about last night? Or that I absolutely plan to do it again?

The morning moves on at a steady but easy pace. I help match customers to treasures for their home and work on a display with one of the local artists for a new series they've brought to the shop. It's a beautiful art deco series based around a woman and the moon. The different pieces correlate the lunar phases and the phases of life from the positivity of youth, with rose tint worked into the pieces. The wisdom and depression that can come with life experiences, with black accents marring the beautiful gold trying to break through. You can see the woman that once was trying to peer through the muck that is now weighing her down. I tear up a little when I think about how this speaks to my own experiences, but I quickly shake it away. These pieces are beautiful. I hope the series sells as a set. Your life shouldn't be viewed in pieces but as a whole.

The lunch hour rolls around. I'm locking the shop door as Krista taps her foot impatiently on the sidewalk. "You're acting like I have daytime TV-worthy gossip to tell you about myself, but you are going to be very disappointed," I say. She smirks at me in response, and we walk down the path toward Dripping for Your Pleasure, the local coffee shop and café just up the block; it's owned by our friend, Willow. The coffee shop is about a 10-minute walk and the weather is pleasant. There is a little brisk breeze, and I just want to lift my face into it. This is a great lunch spot for us. The coffee is rich and bold, and they have these cute little charcuterie style lunch kits, my favorite has fresh blueberries with rosemary crackers.

Willow gives all the drinks and treats clever names. The inside vibe is very dark and gothic. Black walls with dark red textured ceiling tiles. The benches at the tables on the inside are a mix of red leather and velvet. There are black filigree sconces with gold electric candles on the walls. The pictures on the walls depict a mixture of old Hollywood and vintage monster movies. Mareux is playing softly in the background. We get our drinks and lunch then take up our usual booth in the back far corner. It gives the feeling of privacy. I take a drink of my coffee, plain latte with extra foam (it's called a Basic is for Bad Bitches on the menu, giggle), and come away with the milk froth all over my nose and lips. I lick it off then remember I'm sitting with Krista, so I take my napkin and wipe the rest of my face.

Krista is staring lasers at me with her arms crossed. "Spill it."

I stuff blueberries and crackers into my mouth to buy some time. Krista reaches over and takes my plate with a scowl. "Okay, fine! I chatted! You got me!", my mouth still full of food, I cover my face with my hands to keep from spitting crackers at her. Krista sticks a finger in my face "Ah ha!! I knew it! I need all the dirty details. What was his screen name? What did he say his dick size was? Did he share pics?"

"Okay wow, you need to slow down, and the answer is NO to all those questions. It was nothing big." She doesn't buy my downplaying, doubling down on the scowl she continues to hold my lunch hostage. "Fine! I feel kinda like a disgusting creeper but also kinda good. The website is called "Good Finds", I made a basic profile, and I did end up finding someone to chat with and practice flirting last night." She pulls a smirk. "Just flirting huh?" Krista waggles her eyebrows at me as she takes a sip of coffee. "Nothing else?" Mother fucker. "I may have got off." I mumble that last bit into my coffee even though I know what's coming. "Yes!!!!!!!! Girl, I need to know, tell me everything he said!!!"

Now that I am completely humiliated and Krista has pulled every nasty detail from me, we walk back to the shop. Krista literally skips next to me blabbering on and on about being right and how much happier I'm about to be. "You deserve it you know." She turns to me, placing her hands on my shoulders. "You deserve to have fun. You deserve to be happy and feel sexy, valued. You deserve love. You are not used up." She is a total pain in my ass with how well she reads me, but in moments like these I am overwhelmed with how lucky I am to have my best friend. "Thanks friend." I smile back at her.

Our sweet friend moment is interrupted by customers coming toward the shop. I unlock the front door, allowing them in. Busying myself with tidying shelves where items have been rearranged from shop goers looking around, I'm arranging a shelf of used books when the front door chime goes off again. I look up to greet the newcomer when I see Scott swagger in. Again, he is dressed inappropriately for the weather, like he came from the Christmas tree farm. How is he not dying in all those layers of clothing? He is almost like a caricature of an outdoorsman, like if the Brawny paper towel guy owned a sporting goods store.

I inwardly roll my eyes but put on a smile and welcome him into the shop. "Hey Jolie baby, I came by to see if you thought about that coffee date." Oh great, he really isn't going to give up. Krista raises her eyebrows at me from the other side of the counter and tilts her head in silent suggestion I go for it. Maybe she's right. I could practice a little on Scott and bonus, when he sees how awkward I am it will nip this coffee date business for the future. "Um, yeah sure Scott. I'm free tomorrow at lunch, how about then?" He grins what I'm sure he thinks is a panty melting smile and nods his approval at my response. "Yeah, tomorrow is perfect. I'll stop by the shop and pick you up right at noon. You ladies have a wonderful rest of the day." Before he walks out, he runs his hand down my upper arm and winks at me then turns to go. I shudder a little at his touch.

There is just something cringy about him I can't quite put my finger on. I think it's the way he seems to expect acceptance from me, like I should just go along with whatever he says cause he's a man. I love the idea of a man being confident and direct. Scott gives the vibe of a man masquerading as in control but really, he is a complete child when he doesn't get his way. There is something slimy about the way he says my name. I hope agreeing to this coffee is uneventful and puts an end to his interest. I've already had a man who was selfish and controlling. Not looking for a sequel to that.

After work I lock the shop's back door. Krista and I walk together to our cars. The remainder of the afternoon I've been quiet and absorbed in paperwork, dealing with invoices and balancing client accounts. I buried myself in the work to stay out of my own head about tomorrow's coffee date. Barf. Krista is dragging her feet through the gravel and gently kicking rocks. "You don't have to go to coffee with Scott if you're not into it." I look up to face my friend's concerned eyes. "If you really aren't ready, I can cover for you. Or, and especially, if you are just saying yes to him to get me off your back. I don't want you to make a step you're not ready for because I'm giving you shit." I smile back to reassure her.

Straightening the shoulder strap of my laptop bag, I sigh and say, "No, Krista it's okay. He asked again last night after we ran into each other at the grocery store too. He isn't going to stop until he gets a yes. I want to get it over with and then he will move on. Coffee at Dripping for Your Pleasure is a safe outing, and I can send you a 911 text if it gets weird." We both laugh. Then Krista deadpans me with a serious look and declares, "Jolie I will set the store on fire if I need to get you out of a bad date." I smack her on the arm. "The fuck you will! Light his store on fire not mine!"

I drive home reflecting on my day. I'm having some apprehension about the coffee date tomorrow. There is just something off about Scott. His swaggered body language gives off the illusion of confidence but in a pushy way. It's as if he needs to show people he is confident and manly rather than existing as himself. A fake bravado. The tone of his voice when he tries to use pet names with me feels condescending too. If I could fashion the perfect man for me, he would be confident and directive without having to show it off. It would come naturally to him. I would feel compelled to please him simply because his existence would bring me peace and security. My chest gets tight as I recall my heartbreak over my marriage. I never felt secure, always on edge and feeling like I was trying to resuscitate something that was continuously coding.

No, my ideal man would never make me feel that way. He wouldn't need to reassure me with words either. His actions would make me feel safe, desired, cherished. Do relationships like that exist? Maybe only with pets and pet owners. I unlock the door of my little home and BB is there waiting for me like it's been 1000 years since we last saw each other. I could hear her little excited whines through the door as I approached. She gives me a little welcome bark that's gruff and raspy. I got BB from the rescue society right after I left Gary. I was at the farmers market wandering through the vendors when I saw her.

She is a small golden retriever, probably the runt of her litter. She was found running down the freeway dragging her leash. Somehow, she had broken away from her owner and made it onto the roadway, her leash had gotten tangled on a guard rail, and she damaged her vocal cords by pulling against it to get free. I'm sure she was terrified with all the busy cars flying by on the road. A good Samaritan got her free and brought her to the shelter. Her owner couldn't be located so she was placed up for adoption. I fell in love with her immediately.

I call her BB for short, but her full name is The Beautiful and Talented Bea Arthur because of her raspy little voice. I set down my purse and keys on the entry way table, trading them for her leash. I wonder sometimes how she got away from her owner because she is a very polite girl with her walks. She sits calmly to be leashed and doesn't pull when led down the sidewalk. When I first brought her home, I worried about walking her. I have a small yard with a fence and the home I bought already had a dog door allowing access to the yard. I would sit outside with her and lay the leash on the ground next to us and wait for any signs of anxiety she might have about it, but she never seemed afraid. In fact, she would get excited when she saw it as if she was enjoying the thought of a walk.

We stroll down the neighborhood sidewalk together. She sniffs along the ground at sprouts of primrose and into the breeze. No care in the world other than fully embracing the now. I'm jealous. I wish someone would leash me up and take me for walks. Imagine being so secure and connected that you can give 100% trust to that person. BB doesn't care where I lead her, she is just enjoying my company and all the sensory experiences of being outside. She trusts me for food, water, affection. She knows I'll give her every-thing she needs to feel loved and protected. Pets have it so good.

We get back to the house and I fill up BB's water bowl and top off her food. I put away the leash and go about my nightly routine tidying up around the house a little and making a bowl of fruit to nibble on while scrambling some eggs. I toss BB a few of the baby carrots I bought at the store the other evening. At least she likes them, maybe they won't go to waste after all. After we've eaten and I've cleaned up the dishes I go to start my bubble bath. I sink into the boiling hot water and take a sip of pinot.

I've been wearing the kitten ears from my Halloween costume all evening, it just feels right. And anyway, what I do at home alone isn't really anyone's business. They're fun and make me feel good about myself. I don't want to keep being sad; being stuck in the past. I reach over to the laptop to open "Good Finds" and login. Maybe distraction can help me break this cycle a bit. I sip my wine as the message notifications rack up. Scrolling through the names I don't see *Justin_84* again. Guess he wasn't looking for a repeat. Most of the other messages are a mix of *hey baby, I bet you have a pretty pussy* and *sup dawg*, there is one that catches my interests, even if the screen name is a little cringy.

I hover over the message from the other night..... FirmD_m40.... a little green dot next to his name shows he is currently online. Is that screen name supposed to allude to him having a hard on? The profile is to the point, no frills. His profile picture is an artistic black and white photo of a man in a suit, the image is over exposed, so his face is slightly obscured. It says he works in data collection and management, whatever that means. I read that as, boring corporate job. Looks like he lives in some big city a few hours away. I click on the message indicator to open it.

FirmD_m40: Sub?

He wants to know if I'm submissive? I think the answer is yes. Naturally I am the submissive one in my relationships, but I've never done it formally under a D/s situation. Ohhh, maybe the D is for Dom, like he's a firm Dom. That's less icky than announcing a hard on. Something in my subconscious perks up at the concept. I feel — I don't know how to describe it—like, in the sleepy state when you hear your alarm clock, you aren't fully awake yet, but you know consciousness is coming?

SwtJolie: No Sir, but I would describe myself as sub-curious.

FirmD_m40: Explain

SwtJolie: I've never experienced a relationship with a Dom, but I have always felt I had submissive tendencies. Sir.

I try to think about all the smutty dark romance I've read. I am fully aware those books are not accurate depictions of D/s but maybe I won't sound like a complete idiot here.

FirmD_m40: Ah, I see. So, no training then?

SwtJolie: No Sir

FirmD_m40: Tell me more about yourself. You said you had submissive tendencies. Tell me about your past relationships.

I begin giving account of my relationship with Gary, not sharing names or other identifying information because... stranger danger. I find myself unable to stop the tumble of words explaining my anxieties and lack of control I had with him. That I'm looking for more stability and clear boundaries for my future.

FirmD_m40: You poor thing. I'm going to help you find yourself sub. I think you'll find the power exchange of this type of relationship soothing for anxiety. You'll always know where your Dom stands, and there will be clear outcomes when expectations aren't met.

SwtJolie: How? Sir

FirmD_m40: I will train you. But there are rules to this, expectations. For you and for me. Like I said, it's a power exchange.

SwtJolie: What kinds of rules Sir?

FirmD_m40: First you will always address me as Sir, you're already doing so well at that. I will be the only Dom, or man in general, you will speak with.

SwtJolie: Yes, Sir I understand.

SwtJolie: May I ask a questions Sir?

I wait for what feels like an eternity before he responds.

FirmD_m40: You may

SwtJolie: Will this be just this evening or an ongoing communication Sir? And if so, just here on Good Finds? I'm not really looking to meet someone in person right now.

FirmD_m40: Tonight, and ongoing sub, you are mine now. I will tell you when to be here waiting for me, we'll only talk here on Good Finds, for now.... tell me what toys you have sub. Let's start out with some fun.

Uhhhhh I have tons, I have literally everything they make, eekkk and now he wants to know the inventory??? Is he going to assume I'm this dirty horndog? Some items I have because Krista made me get them as a joke/serious "you need to work on your sex life" thing. I'm sure unabashed honesty is the best policy. If he is scared off by it then, better now than down the road. I detail my list for him, slut-shaming my own self as I go. It's so much worse seeing it typed out on a screen.

FirmD_m40: My, my...this little pet has quite the selection. That's very good. It means we can get creative during our talks. Go get your large anal plug and insert it. Let me know when it's done

SwtJolie: Yes Sir

Shit, starting with the hard stuff huh. I know I could lie. I could type dirty responses and pretend that I'm following along. I could just close the website or block him. Or...I could take a risk. I could see where this leads and have fun. I could just let go of all the social standards that hold me captive and let myself have this sexual revolution, in the safety of my bedroom. Who would know? Okay, maybe Krista with her psychic abilities. But who else? It's not like anyone can see me. And it's not like I don't get down and dirty with myself when I need a release. I'm not doing a cam-girl escapade, I'm masturbating in the privacy of my bedroom. He can imagine anything he likes on his end of the computer screen and we both can enjoy this experience for as long as it last. #YOLO

SwtJolie: I've inserted it Sir

FirmD_m40: I want you to take each of your nipples in your fingers and twist and pull them. Pull until your breast stretches.

SwtJolie: Yes Sir

FirmD_m40: Good, again.

SwtJolie: Yes Sir

FirmD_m40: Now use your fingers and rub them on either side of your clit, alternating this with circles.

This is getting tricky to chat and do as he wants, but I juggle it somehow. I slowly circle my clit. My toes curl as I switch between circles and rubbing up and down over myself. I imagine him sitting across from me on the edge of the tub, watching the show. His tie loose around his neck, top buttons undone, his shirt sleeves rolled up his forearms. Ohhh maybe he has forearm tattoos, that's so hot. Maybe he would lick his lips in delight. Maybe he would reach down into the water and play with the plug while I work my clit for him.

SwtJolie: Yes Sir

FirmD_m40: You are doing exactly as I say sub?

SwtJolie: Yes Sir

FirmD_m40: And why is that sub?

SwtJolie: Because you are Sir

FirmD_m40: Good girl, are you getting close?

SwtJolie: Yes Sir

That something in my brain, that floaty feeling from earlier is getting stronger. I feel my brain click off and I enjoy just being in the now and enjoying the sensations, imagining his voice in my ear. I don't have to think, just follow.

FirmD_m40: Why do you need to hold off sub?

SwtJolie: Because you told me to Sir

FirmD_m40: True, and why is that?

SwtJolie: Because you're in charge Sir?

FirmD_m40: Yes I am pet, and therefore I am in charge of your pleasure as well. You cum when I say you can.

Time passes slowly and I feel like a bomb about to go off....how do people actually hold out like this?

FirmD_m40: You may come sub

SwtJolie: Fuck, thank you Sir

FirmD_m40: Very good. Get yourself clean and go to bed sub, oh and drink a full glass of water. You will be here again tomorrow night at the same time.

SwtJolie: Yes Sir.

FirmD_m40: Pet, you can play but cannot cum again until I've given permission. But feel free to edge yourself all you want. You understand?

SwtJolie: Yes Sir. I understand

FirmD_m40: Good night sub

SwtJolie: Good night, Sir

I lean back just resting for a moment trying to get my brain back online. Okay let's think through what I just agreed to. I agreed to consistently meet up online with this stranger and let him be in charge of all my orgasms, essentially. The idea of having a Dom is exciting but I need to think about internet safety. He didn't ask me for any identifying information like my location or name. He didn't demand pictures.... when I said I had a boundary for meeting in person right now, he was fine with that. I feel more comfortable thinking through it. The edging suggestion is gonna be a no for me. There is no way I can do that without cumming, I do not have the self-control for that.

I take a deep breath again. I feel like mushy ice cream, relaxed and melty. I swallow the last of my wine and get cleaned up. I feel a little floaty going to bed. Why is going to bed so much easier because someone else told me too? I try to imagine Scott in this role, and it makes my skin crawl. There is no way he could put me to bed like this. I look at the clock next to the bed, its about 3 hours earlier than I would normally be ending my night. Guess I'm getting my beauty sleep tonight. I set the laptop on the dresser and pad into the kitchen. I fill a glass of water and top off BB's water bowl as well. She looks up at me with her cute puppy grin then happily laps it up. "Sir says we gotta stay hydrated girl. Bottom's up."

My bedsheets feel cool and welcoming as I slip beneath them. I wonder if I'll lay here for hours or fall right to sleep? BB is snoring in her bed, perfectly content. I kinda feel that way too. I gaze in the direction of the laptop on the dresser, the screen is off, but it looks like the power is still on. I need to figure that out. I fall asleep quickly and without perseverating on my romantic failure all night... it's peaceful for once in a long time.

Seeping slowly into the fog of dream state, I open my eyes to a world of skewed colors. I'm a cat again. Instead of wandering in an alley and drinking out of puddles, I'm cozied up in a blanket. It feels so warm and soothing. The dream shifts... it's not a blanket anymore. I'm wrapped in someone's arms. Being held and stroked in slow languid affection while their rhythmic breath ruffles the fur on my head. There's a fire in an ornate mahogany and river stone encased fireplace. The emotion in the environment is soothing, safe. I'm content and I know I'm loved. I tip my head back to rub the edges of my mouth along my keeper's chin.

CHAPTER 5
NEVER ENOUGH

Sir

I'VE GROWN BORED IN the shadows. My routines bore me now. Waking up every day to the same bullshit bitterness of revenge work. Hacking used to thrill me. It was an adrenaline rush to see how much I could push; how fast and deep I could get under people's skin. It's too easy now. I've gotten too good and repeatedly obtaining blackmail for hire has become mundane. But my little pet — she inspires me — ka blank canvas for me to turn into a masterpiece. I could mold her into my perfect pet; train her. Yes, I like that idea. I'll be training my sweet Jolie.

Once I'm satisfied that she is asleep, I close my laptop with a smirk. I feel like a little kid who just found $20 on the sidewalk. My sweet kitty. I've been alone for too long. Giving all my time to business, I haven't allowed myself the luxury of a serious relationship. It's only been a few conversations through a computer screen but — I can't help myself — the intrigue she sparks within me.

Her life and her qualities are so different from mine. She is dog walks, band t-shirts, and hipster shops. I'm business suits, shadows, and cold hard data. But I can feel the obsession rising in me, really it was there from the moment I saw her at the pawn shop. Fantasies of her properly dressed spur me on; the ears on her head, begging to be scratched, her body begging for my pets. Her lounged across my lap enjoying belly rubs and purring with delight.

The privilege of watching her without her knowledge validates my presumptions of her submissive nature. A person is their true self when they think they're alone. If this is her submission when she believes I wouldn't know any better, I can't wait to see her in action when we are finally together. Finally, together — patience is not a virtue I was ever blessed with, the yearning to be with her consumes my mind. Lustful urges to dominate her, to own her — the desideratum for her to be dependent on me for her every need be it physical, emotional — sexual.

It will come in time. It's obvious how much she needs a keeper. Without my direction, she wouldn't eat well, sleep well, or love herself well. The night I found her she lay rotting in her tub writing ugly words on herself. I'm going to fix it though. Like a stray I found soaked from the rain, crying alone, abandoned in an alley — I'm going to teach her what home feels like, what being cared for feels like.

My own pursuit of sleep tonight is fruitless. I toss and turn until just after midnight when I give up altogether. I can't seem to let thoughts of a sweet little kitten go. I feel restless. Maybe I need to work? Be busy. I need my mind occupied by something else. But I'm consumed with the possibilities. My cock is rock hard again.

I wrench the tangled sheets from my legs so hard they dislodge from the mattress. Sitting up on the side of the bed with my head in my hands I contemplate my sanity. Thoughts of a little kitten on her knees, mouth open waiting patiently for direction plague my mind. This distance between us pisses me off and rational thought loses all its appeal where she is concerned. Breaking into her house and slipping into bed with her is sounding better and better. I could be standing next to her bed right now, stroking my cock so close to her face that I can feel her breath on my shaft.

I twist the shower nob on then step back to discard my sweatpants. I picture her little tongue lapping up milk as I rub the head of my cock with my thumb and squeeze the shaft. Precum already weeps from the tip. The hot water cascades over my face and down my nose; fat drops trickling off and landing right on the head of my cock. Each drop hits in time with my imagination of the swipe of her tongue.

I shift from thoughts of her licking milk to thoughts of her licking cum like it's decadent cream. Ass up in the air, tail swishing side to side. Standing over her stroking my cock as I watch her get every drop like the greedy little girl she will be. She'll lift her head to look at me and there'll be cum smeared over the tip of her nose and her cheek from where she's made a mess in her fervor. I splash cum all over the tile as my thoughts run wild. I absolutely intend to recreate that moment with her. I clean up and decide to hit the gym early. I'll need to keep busy or else I'll be sporting a perpetual hard-on until I get back to my pet.

With the files completely copied and unencrypted, I can begin summarizing the findings for my client and turn the report and obtained files over to her lawyers. Then I can give my full attention to my new cause. I slide my chair around to the other side of my desk and open up windows on the two monitors. Running scanning software, I search for keywords such as the congressman's name and financial amounts. Peterman kept meticulous notes, making my job much easier. The evidence details an elaborate real estate scheme. The congressman would front the money for the purchase of some local business to make Peterman look like a legitimate local business owner looking to expand.

Peterman would obtain new leases on one or more properties with his impeccable (fake) credit and down payments. Then, Peterman would sublease the properties, marketing them as forerunner locations for economic booms in the area, offering a discount if one year's lease was paid in full. He then would skip town with the cash and leave the sub-letter with nothing. The original business that was actually purchased would suddenly meet a demise (i.e. burn down) and the insurance payout would go to an offshore account. The congressman gets the payout, and Peterman keeps the lease payments. Peterman changes his alias every time to avoid a trail. I guess when you have a powerful congressman in your pocket it's easy to get a new identity every few months.

He almost didn't qualify for the last business purchase due to my efforts to track him down. A mistake on my part, he got skittish and went off the grid for a while. But if this is the pattern and Peterman stashed the laptop in the local pawnshop, then he might be trying again here in Fayetteville. I switch computer screens and start researching recent business sales in Fayetteville and the surrounding areas.

I make a note to hack the records of Frank's Steals N Deals to see if he comes back for the laptop. It doesn't take long to find a perfect decoy business that I bet is Peterman. No Boundaries; it's a sporting goods store in the same area as my pet's shop. Peterman has this stupid pattern of alliteration in all his fake names. Scott Smith is the new owner of No Boundaries, previously called Ricky's Outdoor Goods. I wonder if this is the same Scott who was in my pet's shop asking her out for coffee.

I continue my search for as much information on Scott Smith as I can find. There's not much of a digital or financial footprint.... I can tell from the generic information that's available that this is a fake identity background. The style they use for witness protection. Same as all his other aliases. It makes sense the congressman's contact for creating Peterman's new identities would be someone with government connections. I check the clock; this will have to wait, I have a date with a sweet kitten.

Her alarm clock is blaring, and she is bashing around her nightstand to shut it off. Poor thing, still so sleepy. She probably has a bit of recovery to do after keeping such terrible sleep habits for so long. Don't worry, sweetheart, it will get easier. Once she acclimates to waking up though, I see she is more enthusiastic with her morning routine, and I love the addition of her purple lipstick.

Pet takes us to work. She has me sitting on the main counter facing out into the store so she can quickly move from working on accounts to helping customers. I like this, it allows me to watch over her and witness her daily, normal, life. I would waste here on the other side of the screen watching her for the rest of my life. She seems to be alone in the shop today though, I wonder where Krista is this morning. Her day may be hectic, but she handles it with grace. I admire her investment in her customers. Taking time to hear what they are looking for and showing them around. I take a break to meet with Lawrence and Davis over the results of the Roberts case and get caught up on theirs.

I'm whistling as I head into the meeting room. Lawrence and Davis are my only employees. Trust in many is hard to muster when you are in this line of work. Lawrence, my number two, is already set up and waiting for our morning briefing. I saunter into the room, take a seat in my usual chair, and kick my feet up on the oval conference table. Lawrence smirks knowingly in my direction. He knows I've been sniffing around a woman, but he doesn't know the extent of my efforts. Davis gives Lawrence a look then not so subtly clears his throat. Great. Those two gossip worse than old women. If they want details straight from me, they'll have to gather up their balls and ask outright.

"Morning. I have all the preliminary intel on the next account."

"Wonderful, Lawrence, I know the client will be pleased with an expediate acquisition on the requested information." I use my best formal boss lingo. He bursts out laughing at my bullshit and then salutes me, "Yes Sir."

Hmm that brings my thoughts immediately back to my new pet. I hurry through my brief on the Roberts case, no need to drag this shit out. I don't have any pressing cases at the moment, now that the Roberts case is mostly settled. I think I'll take some time off to dedicate to my new adventure. I close the meeting, holding the door for Lawrence as we exit the conference room.

"Oh, and Lawrence, I'll be working on a side project for a while. You can handle things in my absence, can't you?"

"Of course, you know you can count on me.   Anything you need done; I'll see to it. You know that man."

"Perfect." It really pays to have close colleagues you can trust. Big firms with countless employees don't give you trust and loyalty. I hand-selected Lawrence and Davis and recruited them to work for me after I did a thorough background check of course, I've never had regrets. We have each other's back, always. I could trust them with my deepest secrets and have become close as brothers. That's why I don't give a fuck about the shit-talking I know they are doing behind my back right now.

I barricade myself in my office for the next few hours with instructions that I'm not to be disturbed. My favorite show is on after all. I'm just getting comfy when I'm suddenly filled with so much rage, I almost launch my computer right through the wall. That dick head Peterman (aka Scott Smith) came in and asked her out. There's no way to truly know if she was interested because I couldn't observe her body language, but her voice was placating and unconvincing.   I couldn't get a full view of them from the laptop position, and she doesn't have security cameras in the store. That will have to change.

She seemed reluctant to say yes to the coffee outing. I can hear the jingle of the little door charm as they leave the shop and the deafening sound of the lock turning into place. Fuming I bang both my fist onto my desktop. FUCK! The ruckus causes Lawrence and Davis to come running. It doesn't matter that I've asked to not be disturbed, nothing could keep those nosey fuckers out with the all the fuss I've made.

"What happened?" Lawrence is the first through the door. I make a mental note to take his BioScan key off my personal office door. "Nothing, I just lost my cool for a second, but I'll feel better after I bash in that asshole Peterman's face." Lawrence looks over at the computer screen, confused by the view of what looks like knick knacks and glittery rocks in a dimly lit room. Davis approaches my desk, putting things together a little quicker than Lawrence. "He move'n in on your girl?" I repeat a mental mantra —these are my friends, they are nosey and meddling because they care— "How do you know anything about my girl, Davis?" I ask through gritted teeth. I fist my hands into my pockets, so I don't pound the table again.

"Look, I know you think you're super stealthy, but you've been twirling around here like the Little Mermaid ever since you located Peterman's computer. We all have access to the case file. Once Lawrence and I saw the woman who bought the laptop from the pawn shop it was easy to put it all together." He shifts nervously from foot to foot, probably sweating under the hate gaze I'm sending him. "You've been spending all your time on surveillance." He gives the last word air quotes, fucking air quotes. He continues because he has a death wish. "But hey man, good for you. We're happy for you. You deserve to find the love of your life. Everyone does." He's looking at Lawrence for backup, but Lawrence is pretending the cup of ink pens on my desk has the answers to the universe right now.

Probably best if I just come clean, they already know, and the longer this drags out the more shit-talking I'll have to deal with from them. We work too damn closely together. With an exaggerated huff and eye roll, I voice the truth. "Fine, you want me to say it, I'll fucking say it. I'm obsessed with Jolie Greenwood, she's mine, and I'll fucking tear to shreds anyone who stands in my way. You got it? Peterman is fucking OVER!" I growl out the truth, admitting my obsession like I'm fucking tattooing it right on my soul. "I would have been satisfied handing him over to Roberts' wife and lawyer, but not anymore. I don't care what favors I have to pull or how much work we, that's fucking right, WE, have to put in... He. Is. Done."

I'm heaving with rage by the end of my rant, but the mental tunnel vision is broken by the sound of a slow clap coming from my right, then joined by another. I look up to see my best friends patronizingly applaud my speech. "You guys fucking suck balls, you know that?" They immediately erupt into laughter, Davis holding his hand out to Lawrence who takes out his wallet and slaps what looks to be a fifty into Davis's palm. "What the fuck you two!" Lawrence just shrugs. "We bet a $50 on when you'd finally crack over this, I thought you'd last at least another two weeks, but Davis said no." Shit, I cross my arms over my chest, not that I would expect anything less than this kind of antic from them.

"So," Lawrence mirrors my stance. "What's the plan boss?" I look from him to Davis who gives a firm nod of solidarity. "We already know where he is, we know what he is up to, it's time to call in some favors and expedite his prison stay."

You might expect me to resort to violence. That's fair. Violence will come. But let's remind ourselves that the pen is mightier than the sword, or in my case, the keyboard. And there are more creative and thorough ways to inflict suffering than simply beating the shit out of someone. I flex my hands repeatedly to dispel the numbness from clenching them in anger while fantasizing about punching Peterman. No matter how much my fists ache to crack Peterman's face open for moving in on what's mine, it would never be an adequate punishment. I want him wretched in agony begging for mercy that I won't give.

It's more than his romantic advances on her, not that he could ever give her what she needs. It's knowing that his interest is insidious; that he only wants to use her as a pawn in his latest scheme. That he will eventually steal everything she has worked so hard for, all the things she's clawed her way to gain as she rebuilt her life after so much suffering. That his actions would cause more suffering. That if he fucks her body and then fucks her life just like Gary did...

I take several slow breaths to calm the black-out rage rising in my chest at the thought of Peterman with my kitty. Cold determination flows through my veins as I rejoin Lawrence and Davis back in the meeting room. Quietly approaching the large whiteboard on the main wall, I uncap a marker and draw three vertical lines dividing the board. We divide and conquer a plan to expedite the take-down of Peterman. Instead of waiting on the drawn-out processes of the legal system, he is about to be rocketed to the front of the line for due process. I have contacts with connections to the FBI, a few phone calls, and a copy of all the dirt I have on him and Roberts is all that will take. Peterman can enjoy a false sense of peace rotting in a cell until I'm ready to deal with him. Next in line is Gary.

Gary Miller, God even his name sounds like a douchebag. I need to wait to make my final move on Peterman, but I can exact my rage on Gary now. Seeing my sweet kitten covered in eyeliner from head to toe; marking her body with self-hate because of what he did — I'm going to burn his life down, literally. He isn't hard to find because the idiot is all over the internet. He enjoys porn, expensive watches, and cheating on his new wife. Of course, Gary has a substantial amount invested in Bitcoin. I bet you've been putting off donating those profits to charity, let me help you with that Gary. I hack my way through Gary's life.

His computer is disgusting. His phone is almost as bad. Ohhhh what do we have here...a locked private folder full of nudes. Oh, Gary, is that what you have to offer? There are at least fifty dick pics in this folder. Do you know who I bet would love to see that? Your business partners. You know, why stop there? Based on your recent sale of Bitcoin and subsequent philanthropic donation of those earnings, I can tell you are a very generous man, Gary. Let's continue the trend and generously share these pictures with the entire company. Why should anyone miss out?

I step back from the whiteboard and admire my work. Satisfied smirks mirrored from my face and my friends' emboldens my choices. The celebration is short-lived though as my eyes fall on the empty third section of the board. Having set my revenge plans in motion only takes the edge off. The physical distance between my kitten and me is unacceptable. I knew from the start that having her only through the computer screen was never going to be enough, but waiting until she's more comfortable with our relationship won't work.

What kind of owner would I be if I left her to the wolf that's come sniffing? My desires for her were already esurient, but the addition of a threat to her happiness is all the justification I need to push her reservations to the side and thrust us full force into the happily ever after I know is inevitable. She needs my incursion into her life — yes, I'm her Sir after all — she needs my care and attention.

The clicking of computer keys slows behind me; Lawrence leans back in the leather office chair, hands folded behind his head. He nods toward the whiteboard. "We've got Peckerman in column one, and Gary shit-face in column two, who goes in column three?" I look from his face to Davis's before turning back toward the whiteboard. Changing markers because nothing that involves these two shitbags should touch anything of hers, I begin to write a new column heading — Jolie Greenwood.

CHAPTER 6
SCOTT IS A DOUCHE

Jolie

FUCK YOU ALARM CLOCK and your mother's a cunt, but maybe she isn't as cunty as she normally is. I slept better than I usually do. Hey, not getting shit-faced in the bathtub and crying all night might be good for me, who would 'a thought. I make sure BB has everything she'll need while I'm at work and then make my coffee. Licking the creamy froth from the center of the mug, I dance my way back into the bathroom.

Maneskin is playing from my laptop that's sitting on the vanity next to me. I sing along with "Baby Said" as I bop side to side and put my long hair up in high pigtails. I spray it well with hairspray and tease it up a little. I'm feeling a little rocker-ish today. I pull on a Maneskin band t-shirt, leggings, and low-profile black sneakers. I wear the purple lipstick too. I wonder what Scott will make of this. I plan to ride out the lunch hour with as little enthusiasm as I can muster up.

Still singing "Baby Said" softly to myself, I unlock the back door of the shop and cross to the front entrance, turning lights on as I go. Krista is coming in late this morning after a hair appointment to have her pink highlights touched up, but knowing her she might show up with a completely new color and style. Maybe I'll see if she wants to go to the nail salon later.

I can't remember the last time I made any appointments like that for myself. I'm doing good to get to the dentist every 6 months. I make a promise to prioritize myself more. I can't let the heartache of the past suck all the life out of my present and future. Sir pops into my mind. I wonder what he really looks like. Like when his face is sleepy in the morning and he's lounging in pjs instead of looking like a fancy business mogul on a dating site. What does his voice sound like? Does he have tattoos? Maybe he will let me ask some questions tonight.

I pass the art deco lunar series we got in the other day. My eyes land on the full moon piece of the series, representing the present. The woman is in a long gold evening gown, and she is centered over the full moon with her head lifting upward and her arms stretched out like she is funneling the moon's energy into a hug. It reminds me of how I felt walking BB yesterday evening.

Watching her be completely present in the moment. That's what I want to do. Be present and just live, just roll along with life, not fight against it. I set the laptop up on the front counter today so I can multitask with invoices and orders while I work the front since I'm alone in the shop right now. Customers start to trickle in and peruse the isles. I have a new order of bulk vinyl stickers to sort and put out.

About an hour into the morning, I get a message from Krista that her stylist was running behind due to childcare issues and she won't be coming to work until after lunch. I let her know I'm fine at the shop and to take her time. The rest of the morning passes quickly and before I realize it, noon has rolled around. The door charm jingles as the last customer exits, but then immediately jingles again. I look up to see Scott standing at the front of my store. Shit, I forgot he was going to come pick-me-up. I had intended to head out early and just meet him at the coffee shop to make this less date-y, but without Krista, I wasn't able to get away early.

My nerves ramp up and I hustle to get the counter settled so I can leave for our lunch date. "I'll be just a second, Scott."

"I *thought* you'd be ready to go straight away, Jolie baby. You *knew* I was *coming*."

What a douche, like I'm going to drop everything to be waiting for him like a schoolgirl. I have responsibilities. He is a business-man too; he should have some grace for me. "Yeah, I know but Krista called in because her hair appointment is running long so I'm running the shop alone today." I fight the urge to say sorry. I don't owe him an apology, nor an explanation for that matter. I don't even want to go to lunch with him. He doesn't know that, but I hope he gets the hint after this is over and never asks again.

"A *hair appointment*?! She should have planned that better. I hope you are docking her pay for the time lost and extra work she's caused you."

"Uh, Krista and I don't work like that. She has the flexibility to live her life without worrying about me knit-picking the hours. I pay her a salary, not an hourly wage. She is so helpful to me I couldn't begin to think how I would run this shop without her." I want to keep going in defense of my friend. The fact that he thinks he has the familiarity with me to criticize her or how I run my shop pisses me off. *Just get through this hour, Jolie, and then it's over. I* walk through the front door of the shop with my keys in hand, holding the door open to cue him to leave my shop. I lock the front door without saying anything.

We walk down the sidewalk with him on my right, leaving me to face the street side. That was something Gary did frequently that always rubbed me raw. The lady should always be on the inside to protect her from traffic. I take a deep breath and catch the scent of the honeysuckle growing along the fence line. I try to be present in the smells and feel of the sunshine on my face with the light breeze whisking through my hair. I can find contentment in these things to balance the ire I feel in Scott's presence. He is talking on and on about himself, I have no clue what he's said because I've given all my attention to the smells and feel of early summer. When we arrive at Dripping for You Pleasure, Scott walks in first and lets the door shut on me. Another tick on the list of things I dislike about him.

I step up to the counter where Scott is ordering, he looks over to me expectedly. I start to repeat my usual on autopilot then catch myself. I don't want to share any important part of myself with Scott. I don't want my favorite Dripping order to be attached to the memory of this fucked coffee date and his presence. I order a lemon ginger hot tea and a sugar cookie. Willow looks at me like I just sprouted seven heads; I grin back at her enthusiastically. Scott pays for our order, and we take a seat at one of the tables. It's a half booth/table and chair. He sits in the booth side. Like, seriously what the fuck? Did he read a manual on how to piss off women in preparation for this date? The girl ALWAYS sits on the booth side.

I sit down in the chair that was NOT pulled out for me and silently stare back at Scott. I know I felt awkward before and couldn't seem to make conversation, but now I've decided he doesn't deserve my efforts, and I will not help this date go smoothly. He can carry the conversation. We sit in silence until the order comes. He man-spreads across the booth seat and gives me a sleazy smile. His boots press down on my toes. I yelp a little and pull my feet back, if he even notices that he stepped on me he doesn't give a shit. Then the real douchery ensues.

"So, Jolie, you know that isn't a healthy lunch. When we go out next time, I'll have to order for you."

"Oh, no that won't be necessary." Mainly because there won't **be** a next time.

He chuckles, "I can see I'm going to have my hands full with you, Jolie baby." I have no idea what I've done to give the indication that this is an ongoing thing. I honestly can't believe I've given indication for him to have asked me out in the first place. Just then my phone vibrates, and I look to see a text from Krista. It's a selfie of her in the salon chair with her hair up in foils. She is pulling a silly face at the camera.

How's the hot date?

"Oh, excuse me a minute Scott, this is Krista updating me about her appointment."

"Tell her to get her ass back to work. You have other things to do than pick up her slack." I don't even dignify that comment with a response. After this lunch hour is over, I won't have to hear his opinions ever again.

It's like an ice bath. How's the appointment coming? Looks like you might be a while still.

Yeah, I'm so sorry. I hope you haven't been overrun at the shop today.

Not bad. It's just been lonely without your sass. And now I'm in hell on this coffee date. I should have just said no and not even come. He is a complete ass.

Awe that sucks. Need me to light his store on fire?

Nah, if he doesn't have a business to run, he might decide to come over and visit more with all his new free time.

I hear a throat clear and look up to see Scott giving me a scolding look. I know it's rude to stay on your phone during a date, but when the date is so bad... I put my phone down anyway. "Unfortunately, I'll need to cut this short Scott. I probably need to get back to the shop early since Krista won't be making it back before the lunch hour is over." I can tell from his body language that he feels offended. Like I've done something very rude and inconsiderate. Maybe I have by texting and then ditching him. I don't care though. I'm glad for the excuse to leave. I send one more text to Krista.

Hey, stop by Dripping and grab me my usual and bring by the shop on your way in, please.

Haha, it's that bad huh? Sure, no problem. See ya soon as I get done here. Xx

Ur the best!!

I get up from my seat, this time I'm thankful that I'm on the outer side of the table, clean up my napkin, and put my cup on the dish return counter. I thank Willow, who smirks at me. I bet she has been watching our exchange this entire time. I'll get loads of questions from her later. Scott throws his lunch away in a huff and follows me out the door.

Crap, I bet he is going to follow me back to my shop. I speed walk there with Scott hot on my heels. When I reach the front entrance,

I stop and spin around to give him an unceremonious goodbye, but Scott is so close our noses almost touch. I leap back and create much-needed space between us. Leaning my back against the shop door, I have nowhere to go. No way am I unlocking it so he can follow me inside. There is still half an hour before we should open again, and I'm definitely NOT spending that time with him.

Scott leans one arm up on the door frame and gives me his sleazy smile again. I look up and wonder what ever drew his attention in the first place. It's not like I'm new to town or anything like that, we have no common interest or mutual friends…Why now, why is he suddenly so very interested in me? Normally I'm oblivious to other people's interests so maybe there were signs I missed. Could I have accidentally encouraged him in some way? "You know, Scott, I really should get back. I have invoices to settle and some items I need to price and put on the shelves." Scott leans in even closer if that is even possible. I duck my head away from him and his garlic breath, does he brush his teeth with it?

"Okay Jolie baby, I hope you give that Krista a talking to about responsibilities. Now, back to *us*. I'll expect you…"

Before he can finish whatever misogynistic bullshit he was about to say I rush in with, "Okay well bye, see you around." With that I turn, unlock the door, and shut it right in Scott's face, turning the lock back and heading to the back office before he can make any protests. Hiding in the back, I wait until the very last second to open the front entrance for the after-lunch shift.

My customers bring me so much joy, I focus on them to keep my mind off stupid Scott. I love hearing their intentions for using the finds from my shop. It makes me feel connected to them as a community. Satisfied with a good day's work, I walk past the full moon art deco piece again, humming contently to myself. I stare at the woman with her arms out reviving the energy from the moon. I want to feel like that, and maybe today I got a small taste. I walk toward the back office, straightening my purse and laptop bag on my shoulder as I lock the back door and head to my car.

The gravel crunches under my feet and I catch my toe on one of the rocks causing me to trip a little. As I right myself I hear an impatient beep of a horn, looking up to see someone in the little parking lot next to my building. It's a small lot with just seven spaces, which should only include my car at this time of day. There is an F-150 parked next to my car. Fucking Scott is leaning out of the window, waving his hand at me to hurry up. Fuck! I need to get home, walk BB, and get settled for the evening... I have a date with Sir. I wanted to be done with Scott. Looks like he reads social cues worse than I do. My inner self stomps her feet in a tantrum.

I come flying in the door. I'm super grateful right now that I have a doggy door, and BB wasn't home with a busting bladder due to my lateness. She is starving though. She prances around her food dish and puts her head in the way as I try to fill it up causing kibble to go flying all over the floor as it bounces off the top of her head. I can't blame her; I'm about 3 hours later getting home than I normally am. Stupid Scott. First, there was about a 45-minute conversation of me dodging his insistence that he should follow me home to make sure I got here safely. I DO NOT need him to know where I live.

If he showed back up at my business after the disaster coffee date, then I'm sure he would be here all the time. Finally, I convinced him I had several errands around town. Following me home turned into him accompanying me on my errands (which I had to make up on the fly). I finally shopped him into boredom, and we parted ways. I check the time; chores will have to wait. I'm not a messy person; I clean my house every day because it passes the time when you live alone, it's become so routine though I feel a little guilty that I'm skipping tonight.

The time I spent running errands with Scott I would have spent cleaning my floors, doing laundry, or giving BB a much-needed bath.... being off schedule makes me feel like a crazy person. I look around my little home and sigh. It isn't the end of the world if I don't do my chores, but I will definitely lose sleep over not crossing everything off my list that should have been. I log on to "Good Finds" to see that I have a message from *FirmD_m40*. Shit.

My nerves immediately go through the roof. Am I really going through with this? Maybe stupid Scott is a sign that I need to leave men alone. I don't have to do this. I could ignore him, create a new login, and continue without having to interact with him again. But a rebellious part of me really wants to talk to him. I could ghost at any time, right? I think about the woman on the full moon back at my shop. No, I'm gonna enjoy the now.

FirmD_m40: Hello pet

SwtJolie: Hello Sir

"Pet," that word makes my brain go fuzzy. I feel floaty again like I did the other night. I like the idea of being cared for and considered in that way.

FirmD_m40: How are you?

SwtJolie: Honestly Sir, I feel frazzled. I had a bunch of chores to work on, but I wasn't able to get home in time

FirmD_m40: What kept you?

If I tell him about *Stupid Scott* is he going to be angry? Call this off? I don't ever want to be accused of being like Gary.

SwtJolie: I had already agreed to get coffee with someone before we started talking on here Sir. That person did not receive the message that I have no interest in spending time with them very clearly and they showed up at my shop after closing. It took some time to break away from them and get back home.

FirmD_m40: I see. We'll get that sorted out, pet, don't worry. What tasks do you need to accomplish?

What does that mean? How will we sort it out? Is he going to give me some kind of consequence?

SwtJolie: I need to do laundry, cook, and bathe my dog, Sir

FirmD_m40: Would you feel better working on them while we talk?

SwtJolie: Yes Sir, I would

FirmD_m40: All right, pet, let's do chores. You have a wearable vibrator, right? Go put it in while you work.

Sexy chores!!! I could wear the vibrator while I wash clothes and sweep my floor. I've never done that before. I normally use that toy when I'm enjoying a good scene in a book. I rush to the bathroom to grab the vibrator. My hands are shaking as I insert it and turn it on. I'm excited and electric inside. This is crazy, **wild**, I'm having internet sexy times with a complete stranger while I wash my underwear.

SwtJolie: I've completed that task, Sir

FirmD_m40: Very good pet.... now start your laundry

I'm shocked at that. I thought for sure things would go as they did the night before. This is even better though. Having Sir direct me in mundane household responsibilities makes this feel even more real to me. These thoughts are difficult to organize, I can't quite put them into words. Having his concerns, his focus, be on normal life (even though I'm wearing a vibrator), endears me to this dynamic.

SwtJolie: Yes Sir.

FirmD_m40: Tell me more about you, pet, what kind of clothes you typically wear, tell me about your hobbies... interests.

I spend the next hour talking about myself. I'm careful not to say anything that I think would help someone track me down online. It does feel nice, though. I can't remember the last time I felt like what I had to say about my interest felt valuable to anyone other than Krista, Willow, or BB. My circle of friends is super small. Sir is patient and seems to love everything I talk about. I feel warm inside.

I am hyper-aware of the vibrator as I move about my home completing my chores while Sir engages me in conversation. He says little about himself; his sole purpose is to learn about me. I asked him the same questions in return. He said I would learn in due time. Right now, it was more important for him to learn all about me so he could direct me better. My vagina is a soggy mess though and it's getting harder to keep the vibrator in, I have to keep my legs crossed, my clit is throbbing and needy.

SwtJolie: Sir, I have a question.

FirmD_m40: Yes, pet. Go ahead

SwtJolie: Why am I wearing a vibrator right now?

FirmD_m40: To show that your training has begun pet. To remind you that while you are completing everyday tasks, you still belong to me and should do your tasks as if I were there with you.

SwtJolie: yes Sir, I understand. Thank you.

FirmD_m40: Have you finished everything?

SwtJolie: Yes Sir I have.

SwtJolie: I have another question, Sir

FirmD_m40: Yes pet

SwtJolie: Why do you call me pet, Sir?

FirmD_m40: Because that is what you are pet, you belong to me now

FirmD_m40: And because you look absolutely adorable in those kitten ears.

I reach up and touch the headband on my head, alarmed momentarily that he knows. Then I remember that I'm wearing them in my profile picture. I exhale a relieved sigh because for a moment I felt like he could see me. He thinks of me as a pet, how do I really feel about that? Some of my favorite smutty books involve pet play. I enjoyed the concept so much that I took an online test that was supposed to tell you if you have submissive tendencies and what types of kink would most likely interest you.

My results came out to 100% submissive with pet play and degradation as my highest matches for kink. I questioned the degradation bit, but then on reflection, I decided that pet play, in essence, is degrading. But when I think of myself in this role, I don't feel degraded at all. Conversely, the idea makes me feel special, seen.

SwtJolie: I've had an interest in pet play, Sir.

FirmD_m40: Of course you have, Kitten. Tell me, do you still have those ears you can wear?

SwtJolie: Yes Sir, I'm wearing them now

FirmD_m40: You're such a good kitty, strip for me. Sit on the floor on your knees

I get undressed and sit on my knees on the cold tile floor. My nipples immediately harden with the cold. I bring the laptop down to a bar stool so I can continue to type while I'm down here. The vibrator is slipping, and I have to squeeze my core to keep it in, making the sensation even stronger.

SwtJolie: Yes Sir, I am

FirmD_m40: Spread your knees all the way open, as far as you can pet

SwtJolie: Yes Sir

FirmD_m40: I'm going to tell you a story pet. And while I do you will rub your clit the entire time, do not lose the vibrator and you will not cum.

SwtJolie: Yes Sir

FirmD_m40: Let's begin......once there was a sweet little kitty. Her pussy was like a perfect little peach. She would do anything to please Sir. And he loved to give her direction

FirmD_m40: This kitty was told to sit at Sir's feet while he read the paper, and then she was brought onto Sir's lap for a rub since she was such a good girl, being still and quiet while he read.

FirmD_m40: This sweet little kitty got rubbed up and down her body, over her breast, down her slit, and over her tail, but she couldn't stay still like before and earned herself a spank on her peachy pussy.

FirmD_m40: Kitty had to sit on her knees with her mouth open with Sir's cock resting on her tongue until drool ran down her chin.

Then she was allowed to swallow Sir's cock and was rewarded with his cum. She needed a reminder that only good kitties who behave get Sir's cum.

FirmD_m40: Are you a good kitty pet? Are you following your directions?

It took a minute to break from my daydream of his storyline to realize I needed to respond. I can't believe how turned on I am at the thought of doing exactly as he said.

SwtJolie: Yes Sir, I'm doing exactly what you said

FirmD_m40: You need to cum pet?

SwtJolie: Yes Sir

FirmD_m40: Do not cum. you will meet me here again tomorrow night. tell me you understand and will obey pet.

SwtJolie: Yes Sir, I understand and will obey.

I understand that I am going to be miserable for the next 24 hours. Fuck.

FirmD_m40:Very good. Get yourself clean, drink a glass of water, and go to bed pet

SwtJolie: Yes Sir.

FirmD_m40: Goodnight pet, and one more thing. you will be home on time tomorrow. Don't let anyone distract you.

SwtJolie: Yes Sir. Good night, Sir.

I go shower and clean myself; I had made quite a mess. My thighs are slick and sticky from the prolonged wear of the vibrator. I pick my favorite blanket from the basket in the corner of the room. It's a light silvery blue color; like a pale seafoam. It's a light shag on one side and fleece on the other, perfect to snuggle up in through the night. I squeeze my thighs together as I stretch under the blanket and then curl into a ball. At first, I worry I won't be able to sleep like this. I could just reach down and finish myself. How would he know? I don't though, partly because I have a feeling he would know. Also, I want to obey. I want someone else to be responsible for my actions; all I have to do is obey. With that last thought, I drift off to sleep.

Chapter 7
No Boundaries

Jolie

MY LIFE BEGINS TO take on a new cycle. i used to come home every evening and wallow in self-pity and hurt. Now I come home excited to complete all my chores. I walk BB and have my nightly rendezvous with Sir. It's been a nice change. The exception is that Scott keeps showing up at the shop. At first, he came by every evening at closing trying to follow me home. I thought he had finally gotten the hint that I don't want him around, but he has been coming by at random times during the business day too. I hide in the back office while Krista gives him some story about me not being available. It's starting to get creepy.

But Sir is wonderful. Every night he has been giving me a task for the next day. It's like a little challenge to complete for him. The first time he asked me to draw him a picture of a flower. Then I was supposed to find something beautiful in nature, take a picture, and share it with him. Sir said I should always try to find beauty life, even in the smallest pleasures. He is invested in my thoughts and feelings about life, not just getting off. He has encouraged me to look for local events I might be interested in and attend them.

I told him I found tickets to see one of my favorite bands. Krista and I are going to see Maneskin next week. Gary would never have let me see a band like this. Not only was Sir pleased that I was doing something fun for myself, but he also likes this band!! We talked for a long while that night, sharing our favorite lyrics. It's hard for me to pick just one song, but Sir said he loves "Read Your Diary," I've been listening to it on repeat while I get ready in the mornings just to feel a little closer to him. Although, until now I never thought about how stalker-y the lyrics are; oh well.

It was so hot at the estate sale this morning that we all had makeup dripping down our faces by the end. Whoever was managing the property clearly was trying to save a dollar on electricity because they only had fans running and no actual A/C. Krista and I got several interesting incense holders, metal trays, and some small China vases that will be sold at the shop. Krista also found some interesting paintings to use. She takes old paintings she finds at thrift stores and yard sales and adds to them to give them an updated and modern spin. We have some of her work in the shop too. Willow even has a few of her pieces that were updated to include a cute little ghost. They are hanging on the wall in Dripping.

After our morning haul, we all headed back to Dripping for a coffee and gossip. Dripping is closed on Sundays, so we have it to ourselves. Willow brings the coffee over to the booth and passes out our usual orders. I take a lick of foam off the top and sigh with contentment, Dripping has the best coffee ever. Willow settles in on her side of the booth and peers at me over the rim of her mug.

It's a deep blue mug with red dripping down the sides and the image of Jaws in the center. It's perfect for her because I can tell by the look on her face, that she is a shark on the hunt with whatever is about to come out of her mouth next. "So, Jolie, how was your date with the No Boundaries dude?"

I choke on my coffee. "What?!"

"The guy you came to lunch with the other day, he owns the camping store, No Boundaries, right?"

Krista and I die laughing, it takes us an eternity to recover. Willow is looking at us like we are psychos. "Is that really what his store is called?! I had no idea!" Krista gasps out between laughs.

"Yes, it's just down the block and around the corner. You've never noticed it? It has the giant elk head coming out of the awning. It's so ridiculous, we don't even have elk around here."

I cringe, "That is ridiculous and tracks for him. I thought you called him the 'No Boundaries dude' because he literally has no boundaries."

"Yeah, that does fit him. I was surprised to see you two together the other day. When you gave me that bullshit lunch order, I knew it was a busted date."

"You have no idea." I cover my head with my hands in frustration as I start detailing the date and Scott's current behavior to Willow. Krista nods along and corroborates his coming to the shop excessively. Willow takes it all in like an FBI agent reviewing a case file, her face the picture of concentration. "So maybe the rumors are true?" Of course, she has gossip, people talk to Willow over coffee more than they talk to a hairstylist. She sits back against the booth and runs her hand through her blonde hair. "You know he's outbid the leases on two of the shops on the other section of the block, Book Ends and Love Your Skin." Krista wrinkles her brow. "Why would an outdoors store owner want a bookstore or a beauty store?"

Willow turns to face Krista in the booth, "Why indeed? Mrs. Clermont, the owner of Book Ends, came by last week. She said it was probably the last time she would be by Dripping in a while. She was very upset. She said Scott had researched her store and knew she was struggling with the increased rent price when her lease came due. He outbid her for space, and she said he did the same thing to Tara, with Love Your Skin. They have to close and vacate their spaces by the end of the month." She pops a bit of coffee cake into her mouth and takes a slug of latte, "He was nice enough to offer her a sublease though, at an upcharge and one year upfront."

Krista and I are speechless with this news. What a douche. If Mrs. Clermont couldn't afford her new lease of course she couldn't afford another upcharge, and who could pay that one year in advance? Willow continues, "He had been coming around the bookstore almost every day for like a month, just out of the blue. Same thing at Love Your Skin. Mrs. Clermont thinks he wants to eventually own the entire block to make it a hunters' paradise road with all outdoor sporting goods and related stores."

"That sucks! The variety of this little area is so special. Why would anyone want to take that away!?" I'm fuming. Krista turns to me with a grim look. "Jolie, when is the lease on Eclectic & Vinyl due?" It's soon, in the next 3 months, I think. I knew the rent was going up, but I wasn't worried about it. The shop does well, and we have very little overhead. But the idea someone would outbid me and steal my space hadn't crossed my mind. Just the thought that I could lose my dream shop has my eyes welling with tears. "Don't worry," Willow puts her hand on mine. "We will think of something. He won't take us down."

I'm so out of it from thinking about possibly losing my shop that I nearly trip and break my neck when I reach my front door. On the front porch of my home, right on top of my welcome mat, are several bags of groceries and one from the pet store. The receipt doesn't give the account from where the purchase was made. There is more food here than I could possibly go through. I bring everything inside and sort out the cold products, so they don't spoil. Taking out my cell phone while putting cheese in the fridge I dial the number on the receipt and report the delivery mistake. The manager is certain it was to my address; although mysteriously they can't say who made the order.

The same thing happened when I called the pet store. I tried fervently to let them know it had to be a mistake. I have a dog and while BB really appreciated the new toys and treats, there was also a feathered retractable cat wand. I would not have use for that so I couldn't have made the order. Again, there was no trace of the original purchaser, only proof of payment so they told me to keep it.

There have been other odd things happening lately too. Friday morning, I went in early to open the shop and get a jump on some account balancing. There was somebody's gum in the trashcan by my desk and my office chair's height had been adjusted for someone much taller than me. I immediately went to the safe to check the cash we had earned that week. Luckily none of that had been disturbed. Krista and I decided to take turns going to the bank each day. I'm not comfortable having so much revenue sitting in the shop until I figure out what's going on.

I leash up BB and lock the door behind us as we head out for our evening walk. She prances merrily beside me as we make our way down the sidewalk. Humidity hangs heavy in the air and my clothes feel like they are trying to audition for the role of skin. BB shakes her head making her leash jingle loudly in the quiet neighborhood street. I turn my head down to look in her direction and catch a hint of movement out of the corner of my eye. It's the briefest glimpse of a shadow behind a nearby tree. I gasp and turn to fully face the direction I saw the shadow only to see nothing now.

Did I imagine that? Maybe I'm paranoid after all this talk of Scott's deviousness combined with the odd things happening at home and the shop. BB doesn't seem to notice; she happily wiggles her butt down the sidewalk. I take a cleansing breath and thread my keys between my fingers for the rest of the walk. If BB is calm, then it was probably nothing. My eyes must be playing tricks on me, probably just a squirrel.

On Monday I'm at work early to meet Krista. We are in the back office before the shop opens going through our accounts and trying to make a plan to deal with Scott. I don't want to lose the shop, but I can't afford to get into a bidding war for the space. I love this location in the city. It's set back away from the hustle and traffic.

There are beautiful patches of wildflowers every summer along the sidewalk. Birds and squirrels come to visit and this summer, I saw a small bunny in my herb garden out back.

The neighboring shops are a big part of the aesthetic. It's all of us together that make this place so unique. We are a community that helps keep everyone thriving. People come here to wander all the shops together. A large percentage of my new customers are people who find Jolie's Eclectic & Vinyl accidentally because they wandered down from the Book Ends or some other store on the block. We need each other to thrive.

I make myself a note to call the leasing agent this week and see what the proposed increase in my rent will be. Maybe if I re-sign early, I can prevent Scott from being able to haggle over my location with the real estate agency. That feels like a quick solution; however, I know I will have a big drop in revenue if the other shops are replaced exclusively with hunting and outdoor venues. Even if I can save myself from Scott's buy-up, it won't be worth it if the other shops have to leave. Being locked into a long-term business lease could be its own issue if my customer traffic is reduced. Uh! This is a mess no matter what the outcome.

My alarm rings cueing me to go unlock the front door for the morning. I pass the lunar art series. As the moon begins to wane, the woman is trying to push away the coming darkness. Her dress becomes increasingly less vibrant as she too is taken over in shadow. "I see you, and I feel you," I say to her as I pass. After unlocking the door, I grab a bundle of dried rosemary and light the end. I walk down the aisles and let the fragrance coat the shop. We need positive vibes here.

Today has been the worst day ever. Nothing bad happened, but Krista and I are both in a shitty mood thinking about what feels like the inevitable. I know I need to be smiling for customers, but I just can't. Not with my baby on the chopping block. All these happy, curious people shopping around unaware of the impending doom I have sinking in my stomach. I am aggressively reorganizing the used book section when I see a customer who looks lost. I should go over there and check on him. I'm struggling with finding the motivation right now to be nice or helpful. I mentally shame myself because even if I lose the shop in the future, I'm letting Scott ruin the now. Just like I let Gary ruin my present for so long after he left me. Nothing is guaranteed to last forever, that's why people (me, I'm people) need to prioritize their present.

"Can I help you find something, Sir?" He is dressed in a high-end dark charcoal grey suit with a light silvery blue tie. It reminds me somewhat of my favorite blanket. He is attractive but what draws me in is his body language. It's confident without being overbearing. Dominant and sure of himself, which seems odd from my perspective because he looks so out of place in my shop. His hair is cut short and his jawline is speckled with a rough salt and pepper stubble. The urge to rub my face against it sparks suddenly in my mind like a shock from static electricity. Stressing over the future of my business seems to have cracked my sanity.

"Ah, you must be the owner, Jolie, how sweet." He smirks like it's an inside joke as he offers me his left hand for a firm but gentle handshake. Something about him seems familiar but also not.

Maybe he is from the real estate company here to assess the shop before they skyrocket my rent! That would explain the suit and how he knows my name. "Yes, you can help me. You can tell me which is your favorite item in this shop." I look around at my inventory. Everything is my favorite. The sadness of this ending weighs me down. I clear my throat to answer, but the words still come out with a melancholy tone. "I assume this is your first time here." If he is here to scope out the property maybe I can appeal to his emotions. Maybe, I can help him see the value in unique and ungentrified businesses.

"Everything in here is my favorite. It all has a place and a purpose here. That was my dream when I opened this shop. I wanted a place where unique items could coexist. Similar to how art imitates life, I wanted to create an establishment that allowed diverse interests and creative expression to mesh together just as people are diverse" I gasp a little because I forgot to breathe while I was talking. "In fact, that is the value of this entire block. Our unique shops are like their own community, and we offer experiences to the public that you can't have with big chain businesses." The man says nothing. He looks around the shop with a judging expression.

"I see. But I asked which item was your favorite." He's looking at me with an expectant and firm expression. I turn around in a circle until I see the lunar series. Walking over to the wall where it is displayed, I wave my hand underneath the length of the arrangement. "Right now, I would say these are the pieces I'm most attached to. I feel like I understand her." I run the tip of my index figure lightly over the tail of the woman's dress. "Her challenges and perspective change as the cycle of her life changes. That is the nature of life.

There are moments of burden, hardship, heartbreak...and then there is hope and abundance."

I walk down to the final piece in the series. It's another depiction of the new moon, the cycle is starting over. Again, the woman is depicted in a posture that brings the promise of hope. "This is where I'd like to be. The series reminds me that this is a cycle and to get from here to here," I point at the first new moon then to the end of the series at the second, "you have to experience these." I wave my hand under the waxing and waning pieces. "I've known this artist since I opened. She is amazing. I hope whoever also falls in love with this series can afford to buy them in its entirety, I'd hate to see them separated."

He looks over the work thoughtfully for a few minutes. He opens his mouth to continue our conversation, but we are interrupted by the very irritating sound of Scott calling my name. He makes his way quickly through the aisles with his chest puffed out and his brow furrowed. "Hey there Jolie baby, I came to take you to lunch again." Scott leans in as if to kiss my cheek, I try to move my face away, but he puts his arm around my shoulders at the same time and I can't quite escape.

"No, Scott, I don't have plans with you." I know my tone is bristled and I should soften this interaction for the customer's sake, but I am fueled with anger at his nerve. Scott and the real estate agent are sizing each other up. The agent has his hands in the pockets of his dress pants but the strain in his shoulders and biceps looks like he could haul off and bust Scott's nose. I wish he would. Maybe he recognizes Scott and hates him too. Oh no! What if he thinks Scott and I are in this together and it hurts my chances of keeping the shop?! I could kick him straight in the dick right now.

Instead, I reach over and claw my nails into his hand that rests on my shoulder. He lets go with a yelp and glares at me.

I take the opportunity to step back, putting excessive space between Scott and me. I want it known he isn't welcome here. The agent steps forward placing himself between us so Scott can't close the distance I've created. He clears his throat and speaks to Scott with unwavering eye contact. "The shop is closing now; you should be on your way." I wish I had a picture of Scott's face right now. I'd hang a copy in every room of my house. He looks like someone just bitch slapped him, and they did...with words. It was a cool and casual statement of the facts, but it was also a declaration that he isn't welcome, and a line has been drawn. Wow, maybe my speech about how special our block of stores is worked on this guy. Scott glares at me over the agent's shoulder but he leaves the shop without issue.

"Please don't sell our lease to that man!" I almost fall to my knees to beg. "He is going to ruin this beautiful area. I know nothing can probably be done about the locations for Book Ends and Love Your Skin, but please don't let him outbid for any more business leases!" The agent looks back at me with a considering expression. He doesn't really answer me though. He simply nods his head, to himself really, not to me. "Make sure to lock up, Jolie." He holds the door open waiting for me to acknowledge him.

"Yes, Sir. I will."

"Good girl." I stare at where he left for a long moment., that whispered sensation of familiarity tickling at the back of my brain.

Later that evening after closing, Krista and I make our rounds straightening the shelves, dusting, and sweeping the floor. I'm running the duster lightly over a shelf of brass odds and ends when I hit something that snags in the cotton. I pull back to inspect it, finding a small gold bell, like the one you would see on a pet's collar. I don't remember this item and it doesn't look like something I would choose from the yard sales and thrift stores. But I like the sound. I jingle it a few times and smile. Aren't bells good luck?

I'm exhausted when I arrive home. Unlocking my door, I kick off my shoes as I go. The first thing I notice is that my laundry room door is open. That should be closed to keep BB contained while I'm at work. I call for BB worried she could be missing. If she were out, she should have run up to me as soon as I unlocked the door. I see a flash through the window that looks out into the backyard, immediately I'm panicking remembering the shadow I saw from our walk the other night. I rush outside grabbing a butcher knife from the kitchen on my way.

When I get to the backyard my panic is replaced by confusion. It's BB, she is chasing a tennis ball, but I don't see anyone throwing it. I run out into the yard ready to confront whoever is out here. No one. Looking down I see an automatic fetching machine. The kind where the dog puts the ball into the opening and the machine throws it. BB is playing fetch...with herself. Where did this come from? I look around the yard for any signs that the fence has been damaged or that someone has been out here.... there's nothing.

I call BB and we go back inside; I'm super weirded out, but it's about to get worse. My dishwasher has been loaded. My laundry has been folded. My bed made. Not only was the bed made, but it's been turned down with my favorite blanket and the retractable cat wand lying next to my pillow. Completely freaked, I start searching the whole house. Nothing looks stolen or truly disturbed. I contemplate calling the police, but what do I tell them? There was no sign of forced entry. Someone politely entered my house, played with my dog, and did my chores? Fuck.

CHAPTER 8
MY PET, MY RULES

Sir

TODAY HAS BEEN EVENTFUL. congressman Roberts has been in a full rage over the information i gleaned from our spicy chat. He isn't so proud anymore of the full-on nudes in compromising poses he sent me or the naughty words he wrote. Lawyers and "analysts" are working to convince the public that the images and the screenshots of conversations were fabricated. That's okay, I have proof they were sent from his computer. Let him wriggle about like a fish on a line trying to deny what he did. Fight as hard as he wants, he's caught. That's the one golden rule of my business. I never fabricate anything; I only expose what's already there. There's nothing to be mad about when the truth comes out; you made this life yourself. He thinks his career is screwed now, wait until the real estate scam is fully revealed.

Seeing Peterman today with his hands all over my pet was enraging. It took everything I had not to rip his arms right off his body, but my kitten wouldn't have appreciated having blood spatter all over her neat and tidy shop. I have my plans to ruin him in other ways. It's only a matter of time before the police pick him up, so

I'll need to be patient and let the "proper" channels work for now. Then, when the time is right...

I need to deal with the rage I felt seeing him in her space and acting like he had ownership of her. If I can't use violence at the moment, I'll settle for taking care of my sweet kitten. I've been following her around town lately. Tailoring my day to match hers. Enjoying the coffee shop, the smell of honeysuckle outside, quick trips to the little grocery store. While she finishes her workday I go by her house. Take care of chores and play with BB. Then I slip off all my clothes and crawl under her bed sheets.

Laying on my stomach, I bury my face into her pillow. It's a decently comfortable bed but the real luxury is being surrounded by my kitten's sweet aroma. Grinding my hips on the mattress while imagining her generous curves, soft and compliant beneath me. I hold the underwear I took from the dirty laundry hamper up to my face and take a deep inhale. Perfection. Laying in her sanctuary, I feel a reverence take over. The place where my pretty pet experiences her most raw and intimate emotions: fear, sadness, lust.

I wrap the lacy panties around my hard cock and stroke. Picturing her riding on top of me, squeezing her breast and pinching her nipples while she undulates, her soft tail stroking along my balls in rhythm with our movements. When the lace is soaked in my cum, I neatly fold them and place them back in her underwear drawer right on top.

Now to shower. I pass her vanity on my way and see her toothbrush in a little cup next to the sink. I pick it up and swipe it over the head of my cock, collecting remnants of cum in the bristles then replace it in the cup. Her tub is cramped from what I'm used to but it's a cocoon of her essence. I open all her shampoos and soaps, loving the smells of her, while making mental notes of all her brands and fragrance preferences. How many times have I watched her lay here covered in bubbles, massaging her soapy breast with the same loofa I'm washing my cock with right now?

The temptation to jerk off again to the mental image of my cock running between her bountiful soapy breasts has my cock hard as iron. Giving in to the irresistible fantasy, I release myself all over the loofa and her soap bar. When she baths tonight, she'll be covering herself in me. Once I'm finished, I change her bed sheets and turn the bed down for her. Today is laundry day for Kitty. The less time she spends worrying about chores the more time she can enjoy being my pretty kept pet. I look down at my watch to check the time, 4:30 p.m., I should get going. She'll be home soon, and we have a date.

We've been meeting every night. Talking for hours. I don't play with her every time. This dynamic is all-encompassing; it isn't limited to sex. I want her to feel my presence every minute of the day, in every breath she takes. There won't be a thought or action she makes without considering me. I know it's working too because she's been sending me pictures of what she's doing throughout the day. Pictures of her coffee mug full of frothy creamer. Little snack cup of blueberries from the coffee shop. She baked a cake a few days ago and cut an extra slice, served on a separate place setting just for me. I've picked out her nail color, lipstick, and underwear....

Tonight, I need to see her cum for me. I have a little task for her that I plan to exploit later. A list of rules for her to memorize. Later on, when we're finally together we will see how well her memory works under my distraction. I fantasize about the day I will finally have her in my presence. Oh, the things I've come up with. I'm early to log in. While I wait for my little kitten, I busy myself opening the package I received today. It's a little surprise for her.

FirmD_m40: Hello Kitty

SwtJolie: Hello Sir

She's sitting on her bed, crisscrossed, leaning in toward the monitor. Her full lips a ruby red and her ears are a little off-center, adorable. I've noticed she's been wearing more makeup since we've gotten closer. I love her beautiful face either way, but I'm glad to see she has been doing more things for her own happiness.

FirmD_m40: How was your day?

SwtJolie: Okay I suppose, thank you for asking Sir. Things have been interesting lately, I'm not sure exactly how I feel. How was your day?

FirmD_m40: Thank you for asking, Kitten. I rather enjoyed my day. Interesting how?

SwtJolie: It's a long story, Sir, I'm not sure you really want to hear it all.

FirmD_m40: When I ask a question, Kitten, I expect a full answer. You need to remember that, or you'll find yourself with a punishment.

SwtJolie: You'd punish me, Sir?

I grin at the shocked and pouty expression that crosses her face. She can't imagine a punishment administered when we are on the other side of a computer, but that will change, sweetheart.

FirmD_m40: Oh yes, how else will I train you if there aren't consequences?

SwtJolie: How would you punish me if we only talk online, Sir?

FirmD_m40: That is for, Sir, to decide, and you will find out when you disobey. We're getting off track. I've asked you a question.

SwtJolie: Yes, Sir. Some odd things have been happening around my home and shop. I've been finding items that weren't there before and then today it seemed as though someone was in my home, but they didn't take anything, it was like they did my chores. I don't know, maybe I'm going crazy and it's nothing.

FirmD_m40: I see.

SwtJolie: I'm on edge because it seems like someone is sneaking around my personal spaces, but they seem to have good intentions.

Oh, kitty, you have no idea the depth of my intentions.

FirmD_m40: You've been under a great deal of stress lately. Let me help you.

SwtJolie: How Sir?

FirmD_m40: All you have to do is listen to Sir; I take care of you from now on.

SwtJolie: Yes, Sir.

FirmD_m40: I know you're feeling stressed from work and other things. I have some tasks for you that will help. Are you ready pet?

SwtJolie: Yes, Sir.

FirmD_m40: Go find something to write with, for your skin, a marker or eyeliner or something.

SwtJolie: Yes, Sir. I can use my eyeliner.

FirmD_m40: Good. Now I want you to write something on your breast. Write 'Good kitties say Yes Sir'. Tell me when it's done.

SwtJolie: Yes, Sir, it's completed.

FirmD_m40: Now, on your inner thighs, write 'Good kitties get cum'

SwtJolie: Yes, Sir, completed.

Oh my god, watching her spread her legs wide open, a direct view tunneling down her already wet pussy, as she gently writes my words along her thick thighs. I want to die here, suffocated by her legs wrapped around my head and drowning in her cum.

FirmD_m40: I want you to put on the nipple clamps you have.

She leaves my view for a moment then returns with the chain. A pretty gold chain adorned with little pearls and clamps on either end. She could have put it on in the bathroom, but she brought it back to the bed for me. It wouldn't matter, I have cameras in her bathroom now, but still. She licks her fingers and tugs on her nipple then blows softly on it until it's a pretty little peak, pulling it forward and applying the clamp. Her face grimaces with the added pressure.

SwtJolie: I have them on now, Sir.

FirmD_m40: And your ears my pet?

SwtJolie: Yes, Sir.

FirmD_m40: mmmm, I'm sure you look stunning all dressed up.

SwtJolie: Thank you, Sir.

FirmD_m40: I want you to lick your hand then rub it on your face, clean yourself, Kitty.

SwtJolie: Yes, Sir

FirmD_m40: How does that make you feel, pet? To be treated this way.

SwtJolie: It should be demeaning Sir, but I enjoy it, something happens to my brain. I get all floaty feeling and it's a little euphoric. This happens when you praise me too, Sir.

I know, Kitty, I know, I've seen the expression of rapture on your face.

FirmD_m40: Good girl. I want you to enjoy our time together as much as I do.

FirmD_m40: How do your nipples feel?

SwtJolie: Sore, Sir.

FirmD_m40: Pull the chain.

SwtJolie: Now they hurt, Sir.

FirmD_m40: But do you enjoy it?

SwtJolie: I'd enjoy it more if you were the one doing it, Sir.

FirmD_m40: Of course, Kitty. All in due time.

SwtJolie: We've never talked about meeting in person, Sir.

FirmD_m40: I know you aren't ready. That's a conversation for another time. How wet are you? Remember to be detailed for, Sir.

I don't want to scare her off. When we are finally together, I need her to be at peace with what she is to me, to be able to fully submit to it. I want everything from her.

SwtJolie: Yes, Sir I remember, I'm very wet, Sir, I've soaked a little spot on the bed and my thighs are sticky, the eyeliner is smearing a little.

FirmD_m40: Very good. I want you to rub your clit with your paw.

SwtJolie: Yes, Sir.

FirmD_m40: While you do, I'm going to give you rules to follow. You are to rub yourself the entire time. Do not cum.

SwtJolie: Yes, Sir.

Her finger glides easily over her clit, splitting her index and middle finger on either side then spreading out to rub and squeeze her labia. Her pretty blue painted fingernails glistening with cum. She has me groaning out loud with how ridiculously wet she gets.

FirmD_m40: This one you already know. You do not cum without permission.

FirmD_m40: Always use honorifics when addressing your Sir.

FirmD_m40: You will accept correction from your Sir, trusting that he has your best interest in mind and would never cross your limits, but that punishment is not always pleasant.

FirmD_m40: You will remember and will use your safe words when needed, absolutely no reservation about communicating your need to stop something when needed.

FirmD_m40: You will remember to take care of your basic needs when Sir is unavailable to attend to you, such as staying fed and hydrated.

FirmD_m40: Good kitties know their worth and will not bully themselves with negative thoughts or acts.

FirmD_m40: Do you agree to these rules pet?

SwtJolie: Yes, Sir. I do.

FirmD_m40: Good. I want you to memorize these. All good kitties know their rules by heart, so they do not stray from them.

SwtJolie: Yes, Sir.

FirmD_m40: I want you to cum while reciting them Kitty. Record it and save it. I want you to watch this video of yourself cumming to Sir's rules every night this week while you recite the rules along with yourself and cum again. You should be close by now, make sure you don't cum until you say the very last rule. I'll know if you do, pet.

FirmD_m40: After you're done you may remove the clamps. I want you to drink a glass of water and go to bed. You may clean yourself up, but I want you to keep the writing until tomorrow. Tell me you understand.

SwtJolie: Yes, Sir, I understand.

FirmD_m40: Enjoy yourself, Kitten. Goodnight.

I sit back in my leather desk chair and take out my cock. The view from her laptop camera gives front-row seats. I fully intend to spank her ass for keeping it open and pointing directly at her bed all the time, but for now, I enjoy watching her do things like undress and sleep. On the weekends she lays on the bed snuggled with that light blue throw blanket and reads for hours. Sometimes she dances in the mirror to '90s music, absolutely adorable. 69 Boyz "Kitty-Kitty" really gets her going.

Right now, though, right now I'm getting a really dirty show. I have the perfect view of that peachy-sweet pussy. Her legs are spread out like a welcome for feasting. The chains of the nipple clamps shimmer in the soft bedroom lighting, beautiful. She has her phone propped on a pillow by her ankles getting a first-person perspective recording. I'll copy that from her phone later. Ah, the sound of her gasping out my rules, trying her best to say them verbatim, it's like enjoying a symphony. I stroke my cock to match her tempo as she rubs her swollen clit. Imagining I'm there and instead of her fingers running up and down her slit, it's me.

She struggles as she gets to the last line. I zoom in to get a better view of her fingers. Soaked in her own cum; it's running down in a slow juicy stream; framed by naughty words scrawled on her inner thighs. A masterpiece. I can only imagine how good she must taste and smell right now. Soon I won't have to imagine; I can eat whenever it pleases me. She finishes the last line and finally allows herself to cum. I smile with pride at how she's completed her task. My cock is swollen and hot in my hand and I cum with her.

I'll be watching that video on repeat until I get her in my presence for real.

My little kitty lays across the bed trying to recover. That's probably the dirtiest thing she's ever done but that will change, soon. She slowly begins to reanimate, moving her legs around and reaching up gingerly to remove the nipple clamps. She hisses with that; they have been on for a while so I'm sure it hurts to take them off. Her nipples will probably still be sore tomorrow. I should have told her no bra tomorrow, damn. Next time. She sits up slowly and leaves the room to get a glass of water. What a good girl, remembering everything Sir told her to do. She paces in front of the dresser. Looking at herself in the mirror behind me, I assume. I love it; it feels almost like I'm there in the room with her.

So beautiful, her little ears crooked on her head and her hair a wild mess. Her nipples are bright red and swollen. The words I gave her smeared over her breast. I watch her inspect herself and she catches her breath and finishes the water. "Fuck," she whispers and shakes her head at herself. Then a single tear trickles down her cheek, her eyes water up and her nose reddens. She's still talking to her reflection, "He's a man in my computer; why am I always so heartbroken when he leaves?"

She schools herself and sets the glass down on the dresser next to the computer; the click jarring through the speaker. Then she's gone from my view, and I hear the sounds of the shower. I want to burst through this computer screen and hold her. She needs more care than a glass of water and tucking herself into an empty bed. I should be the one cleaning her up, giving her a drink, and tucking her in. I will be. I thought I should hold off a little longer, I thought

I was rushing her. I see now I was wrong. My sweet kitten needs me. I need her too.

When she returns, she climbs into bed and turns out the light. There is still enough light from the bedroom window that I see her silhouette. I watch as she falls into sleep, hyper-focused on the pattern of her breathing, making sure it stays calm, and she isn't crying herself to sleep. Being held at a distance from her is miserable. I want to be everywhere she is. Like an addict, I need another, stronger fix. I need her in my veins.

Peterman. That fucking douchebag. I am one step closer to ruining his life for putting his hands on what's mine. I minimize the screen where I watch my sweet kitten rest and open my email to read a reply from a friend in The Family. His response is short and clear, he's always been a straight-to-the-point kind of man.

Consider it done.

The muffled echo of the opening music blasting from giant speakers follows me through the back hallways of the concert venue. Random concertgoers ask me where the restroom is or how to get to their stadium level. Ugh, it's not really their fault. The security guard getup is what draws them to me. I make it around to the merch table and post up near a pillar to watch my sweet kitten and her friend buy t-shirts. After they put their names in the raffle container and walk away, I approach the counter. "Hey, dude, I need to bring this upstairs now." He barely nods at me as I take the container away and dump the entire thing in the trash bin as I pass by.

I follow the girls up the stadium stairs. With the low arena lighting and the security uniform, I get close to Kitten without her getting suspicious. People will see a security guard and think nothing of it. The hat helps hide some of my face. I sent the info about the girls getting upgraded to the stage manager already and he should have given their names to the band to announce. As the opening rifts are played the lead singer approaches the front of the stage. My kitten and Krista have their arms linked and fingers crossed. When he calls their names, the squeals could shatter glass, and they begin jumping up and down so wildly I'm nervous they're going to go tumbling down the entire level. I hustle over and start to usher them out of the aisle and lead them to their new spot in the pit. Her happiness is infectious, and I'm on cloud nine knowing I put that joy in her face.

Taking a risk, I place my hand on the small of Kitten's back as we turn corners. After getting them settled in the pit, I stick close, watching over the girls as they dance their hearts out. The light show and heavy bass mix together to create an almost tantric atmosphere; sweaty bodies bob and gyrate in time with each other. The dickhead standing behind them starts getting a bit too interested, creeping closer and closer to them. Just as he's about to work up the nerve to fully move in, I clamp my hand down on his shoulder like a hammer and spin him toward the exit. He takes one glance at the security get-up and complies. "Whoa, Dude, what did I do?" He struggles to keep up with my determined stride, my hand still clamped down on his shoulder as we twist and turn through the hallways.

Finally, I reach my destination. "Drunk in public," I grit out just before I shove him through an exit leading to the back lot of the arena. He trips into the alley, his confused expression quickly cut off by the slamming of the exit door back into place. I return to my watchdog post for the rest of the show shutting down any other want-to-be suitors with my death stare. That's my kitty, they can all back the fuck off.

CHAPTER 9
PERPLEXITY

Jolie

I WAKE UP FEELING hungover, but I didn't drink last night. This is an emotional hangover. I feel weighed down again. The urge to write ugly, **hateful** things hits me hard. I roll to the edge of my bed and sit up, letting my feet dangle off the edge for a moment, trying to focus on the movement and clear my head. With a heavy sigh, I walk to the bathroom and over to the mirror. I clench my hands on the edge of the countertop until my knuckles are white. A cocktail of anxiety and grief is churning in my stomach.

Reaching for my eyeliner, I fully intend to write those ugly words. I jerk off the cap and bring the eyeliner toward my chest, ready to mark myself with hate, but when I look up and fully gaze into the mirror, I behold my naked body's reflection and stop with my hand mid-air. I have the words "Good kitties say yes Sir" smeared across my breast. One of Sir's rules comes to mind. *"Good kitties know their worth and will not bully themselves with negative thoughts or acts. Do you agree to these rules pet?"*

"Yes Sir, I do."

Right there across my chest. "Good kitties say yes sir." *Am* I a good kitty? What does it mean to be a good kitty? I feel like a fraud.

I'm falling hard in a relationship with a computer. I am completely obsessed with this man that I have never seen or heard for that matter. Is this how people become prison pen pals? You write to each other and bask in the presented ideals until you fall madly in love? It's so easy, there is no "life" to create stress or interfere with plans.

When you are chatting, you are playing a role. I have been sucked into the ideal of Sir. Surely, he doesn't return my affection so sincerely. This is probably just escapism from his otherwise dull life, looking for an easy thrill to pass his time. Is he using me? Maybe we are just using each other? Am I guilty of the same thing? If I was only using him, would I be so desperate for "more?"

I considered *JustinJ_84* was a creepy old dude living in his mother's basement, Sir could be too. He's never told me anything about himself, even though I've been telling him all about me. That right there should be proof enough. People who are mutually interested in each other want to share their interests and details about their lives. This is one-sided. What if he can't share it?! He could be a criminal, a money launderer for the mafia, or an undercover CIA, maybe he is in witness protection?

Those ideas seem dramatic but either way; *basement loser* or *made man* can't lead to anything serious, real, or long-term. I should have never done this. I need to stay off the site. Ghost him and try to live my life. The mere thought makes my heart race, and I feel gut-punched. Can I quit him? I start to panic thinking of potentially being swallowed up by grief again just like with Gary. My chest is tight. I can't catch my breath. If I feel like this from toying with the thought of losing Sir, what will happen to me if I let this fantasy continue until I'm in so much deeper? I started this so I could get comfortable talking to men again and eventually graduate to dating in real life. Instead, I've developed this irrational attachment to a fake person. That's it. I'm quitting. I'm not going back online. I need to end this.

I go through my morning routine and get ready for work. Back to the sad me that existed before I found Sir. I cried so much that I finally just washed my face and said fuck the makeup. I did leave Sir's writing on my body though, unable to bring myself to remove it just yet. It can wait until tonight to be washed off. BB licks my hand and whines. She knows this side of me and is probably worried that the sadness has returned. I pet her head to reassure her and give her a bacon strip. On my way out the door, my purse slips off my shoulder and knocks over the umbrella stand next to the door. I'm a clumsy mess today. The entire ride to work I war with myself; having a delusional argument out loud like there are two of me riding in the car.

Kitty: I want to be happy; I deserve to be happy, damn it! People have all kinds of relationships. I'm an open-minded person. If Krista told me she had fallen hopelessly in love with a person she had only written conversation with, I would hug her neck and tell her how happy I was for her. I should turn that attitude on myself.

Jolie: I feel dysfunctional though. I have a failed marriage that I have never moved on from, maybe I am clinging to Sir because it's easier to attach myself to this than face my real problem. I never learned to love myself again after Gary. I should deal with that. I should learn to be at peace with who I am now before moving on. But the thought of letting Sir go hhhuuurrttttsss!!!!

Kitty: Fuck that! You can't deny what you have gained from being with him. Your life has changed for the better. You dress like yourself again. You don't stay up all night crying in your wine glass, you haven't perseverated on Gary, you aren't breaking plans with friends, you're hydrated and getting enough sleep...

I begin to sob.

When I arrive at work, Krista is already waiting in the back office for me. I must look like complete shit because her face turns from excitement to concern. "What the fuck happened?!"

I haven't told her about Sir. I can't think of a lie quickly enough before she rushes in.

"Is this about Gary? Don't feel bad for that fuck up. I was coming in here to talk shit about him given the news, I wasn't expecting you to be upset like this over it."

"Whaaattttt are you saying?"

"Girl, you haven't seen?!"

"Uh, no. I don't know any news about Gary. I was just picturing my life without the shop and working with you. That's all." Finally, a lie comes to mind that could be plausible. Krista turns her phone around to a video clip from the news station. It's a report about a man getting fired and coming under investigation for sexual harassment and sharing of nudes in the workplace. IT'S GARY!!!!! "Holy shit!!!" I snatch the phone away from her and scroll through the article. I can't believe my eyes.

"Holy shit is right girl; you dodged a bullet when he walked out on your marriage. Apparently, they were able to trace his behavior all the way back to when you guys were still married. He is a disgusting person and karma finally caught up with him." She dusts her hands together and flicks out into the air for emphasis. I'm speechless, gaping at the cell phone in disbelief. It wasn't that I was surprised he was guilty, I was surprised he had been caught.

Krista disappears for a moment and comes back with a baby bottle of prosecco. "I know we're at work, but this deserves some celebration, bitch!!!" A small smile tugs the corners of my mouth as I watch my friend dance around to her own tune celebrating my ex's bad fortune. She pours each of us a half glass in paper cups from the water cooler. We clink our cups together and laugh at the expense of my trashy, low-classy ex. I love Krista. Thank you, God, for sending her into my life.

After our mini-party in the office, I'm able to get my mind off of Sir for a few hours. I'm flowing in the vibe of my shop and connecting with the people who visit us today. I met Sarah Kate, a college student, who came in to shop our selection of hand-thrown mugs. Her father's birthday is next week. She wanted to get him something unique but also something he could get daily use out of. He happens to also be a geologist. One of the hand-thrown mugs has sapphire geode stone embedded in the glaze. It was a perfect find for Sarah Kate. I wrapped it in tissue with a curling ribbon and put a shop business card on it for a gift tag. Experiences like this make me feel like I'm making the world a better place through small acts.

My mind turns to worry again. What am I going to do if I lose the shop? My stomach is in knots and my chest feels tight. Just breathe Jolie, in and out. The lie I told Krista isn't completely untrue. I know she feels it too, I see the sad look in her eyes. We walk silently down the block to Dripping for lunchtime. Krista trails her fingers along the fence line as I trudge behind her on the sidewalk. Honeysuckle drapes over the fence and grows through the spaces between the iron. I pick two blooms, shoulder-bumping my friend and offering her one. We cheers our flowers and then sip the sweet nectar. Never having to say a word because we both know. No matter what happens with the shop, we can always depend on each other.

❧

Sitting in the booth at Dripping, I run my hands slowly over the velvet fabric of the cushion. If my life is about to change, I want to savor every fine detail I can. It's a slow day at the coffee shop so Willow is able to sit with us during lunch. She has been dying to hear all out the concert we went to, and no one tells a story like Krista. I sip my latte, enjoying the sweet foamy cream on my tongue as I'm transported back to the memory of the concert.

Willow is on pins and needles listening to Krista retell what went down. I wish she hadn't been out of town at the time. She loves Maneskin as much as we do and would have died to be there with us. It was a small venue, which made the show that much more amazing. We were able to be so close to the band. The first thing we did was hit the t-shirt table. We wanted to make sure we got our sizes before they sold out. There was a raffle at the counter. With every t-shirt sale, your name went in the box for a chance to get upgraded to the pit. At first, I told Krista I didn't want to put our names in. I don't mind sitting in the nosebleeds at shows. Krista was having none of it though.

"Picture it, we are sitting in our complete nosebleed seats rocking to the bass intro as the band members take the stage. Then Damiano comes on stage, no shirt, leather pants, gets on the mic, and calls the winners of the raffle! Can you imagine his sexy *Ital-*

iano accent calling our names!!!!! It was epic, to say the least. We were both screaming and jumping up and down!!"

She is grabbing my arm and bouncing up and down in the booth seat, rattling me so hard that I almost spill my coffee. I giggle and Willow grabs some napkins. Kirsta continues her story. "A smokin' hot security guard escorted us down, he couldn't take his eyes off Jolie." She winks at me and grins like a wolf. I just roll my eyes. He was nice looking, I almost felt like I recognized him but...

"Aaaaannnndddd thhhheeeennnn, as if that wasn't enough... at the end of the concert we got pulled on stage and we danced with Victoria during the last song!!! Oh my god, I almost can't believe it. Shit like that never happens to us. The hot security guard was right there basically drooling over Jolie, too." This time she jabs me in the ribs, I aspirate coffee through my nose and almost die right here at the booth. "Uh! Oh oh oh! And then we got all our merch for *FREE* and they refunded our ticket cost. So now the concert, t-shirts, and VIP treatment were all free!!!"

"It was a good night; I hate you weren't with us, Willow," I say.

Willow throws her hands up. "Bitches, I'm never missing out again. From now on, I'm going to every concert you go to. Thanks for bringing me back a t-shirt." We all laugh as the door chimes with a new customer. We turn in unison to look and see fucking Scott walk in. After he came in and tried to kiss me the other day, I told him he was banned from our shop due to sexual harassment. He has been sniffing around Dripping ever since. Willow doesn't have a good reason to kick him out. We are all scared he is going to take our business. I haven't heard anything from the real estate agent since the other day. I tried calling the company to follow up, but they didn't know what I was talking about. I guess that just shows how big and out of touch their business is; they can't even keep track of what their agents are doing.

Scott approaches our table with a menacing look and his hands in fists. "I don't know exactly how you did it, Jolie, but you fucked around with the wrong man. I'm not going to take this sitting down." I stammer on my words; "I, uh, I don't know what you mean, Scott." He leans over to where I'm sitting in the booth with a murderous expression. "Don't you play dumb, you stupid little cunt. You think you can report me and just go about life, no consequences?!"

I push him back with my hand and the three of us stand up from the booth. I suddenly see red. Who is this jackass? First, he tried to date me to get close to my business, and he's trying to take our block, now he thinks he is going to intimidate me? I didn't do anything to him!!! How dare he try to push me around! I hear the words of Sir again. *"All good kitties know their worth...."* I don't feel like just a kitty though, in this moment, I'm a tiger!!!!!

"Fuck off, Scott! And not just a little. Fuck all. The way. The fuck off. If you can't be polite with that shit trap you call a mouth, then take it somewhere else!" I get right in his face too, I'm a lot shorter but I don't give a crap right now. I got my girls at my back, and we are gonna teach him a lesson about messing with us and our block. I feel like such a bad bitch right now, it's exhilarating.

Willow steps forward, arms crossed and a smug expression. "Wow, thank you, Scott." She hardens the "t" on the end of his name as she speaks. "I've been looking for a reason to ban you from my coffee shop. You just gave me a perfect one." She whips the towel off her shoulder and snaps it between her hands. "You came in here and threatened a customer without cause and I have Krista as a witness. So, get the fuck out, and don't you ever come back." She points at the door with a huge ass grin on her face. As he leaves, he turns back one last time, "This ain't over, Jolie." Those words send a chill through me. There's so much virtual in his voice and malice in his expression. My worrisome thoughts are broken when Krista busts out laughing.

"Check it out, ladies." She took a picture of Scott's face when I chewed him out. It looks ridiculous, all snarled up and taken aback. "Send that to me Krista, I'm going to hang it on the wall with a big ass sign saying he is banned from multiple shops on this block for harassment," Willow says. Willow walks over to the door and flips the sign to closed. "Let's have a little celebration ladies." She turns back behind the counter and cranks up the overhead radio. "Today is a good day, all the douchebag assholes are getting what they deserve." She places the little shot glasses she uses for espresso on the counter and fills them up with whipped cream. "To Gary and Scott! May they forever fuck off!" We raise our glasses and take our shots of cream with squeals of girl power.

For the moment, my worries are gone. It's me and my friends, dancing our hearts out to "Boy Problems" by Ashton and taking whipped cream shots in the middle of the coffee shop. Willow finally gives up trying to get the cream in the shot glasses and just starts spraying Krista and me in the face. I feel joy. I feel alive. I'm glad I stood up for myself. Ultimately, my thoughts drift back to Sir. His words had given me confidence and they helped me find a sense of validation I had struggled to find on my own.

Krista and I decided not to open the shop back up for the afternoon. Instead, the three of us ordered pizza and beer to the coffee shop, got day drunk, and then went shopping.

A few days later Krista and I are back at Dripping after the work-day. We have been walking down together to collect Willow after she closes up. Remembering how Scott was showing up after I closed Eclectic and hanging out waiting for me made me worry for Willow's safety now that he seemed to be targeting her. The three of us decided we would leave the block as a group for the time being. It's a shame that this is what women have to do to protect each other from potentially violent men.

As Willow reaches out to flip the lock and the closed sign on the front door she is interrupted by furious knocking. We all jump and scream. The knocking pauses for a moment then continues; accompanied by the urgent voice of Mrs. Clermont, "Willow! Willow are you there honey?!" Willow opens the door to let Mrs. Clermont inside. She is frantic but seems excited not terrified; the three of us trade looks trying to work out what could be going on. "Oh, my goodness Willow honey, thank goodness I caught you." Mrs. Clermont is out of breath and it's still unclear if this is an emergency or not. She continues; "I couldn't wait, I had to come straight on and tell you what happened!" She looks around at all three of us with a grin like the cat that ate the canary. "I got my shop back!!! Book Ends and Love Your Skin aren't going to close after all!"

We gasp in unison. "That's great news, Mrs. Clermont! How did that happen, what's changed?" We gather closer to her waiting anxiously for an explanation that could help us all.

"It seems that Mr. Scott Smith wasn't Mr. Scott Smith. He is a real estate scammer!!! But he's been found out." She pants. "His real name is Jonah Peterman and there is a warrant for his arrest in multiple states. There's an article online about the whole thing! But never mind that for now." She waves her hands around the air and then pulls a rumpled envelope from her purse. "The good news is someone has purchased the block and renewed all the leases without an increase in rates!!!! A certified letter came to my home this morning with the new lease agreement. Isn't that WONDERFUL!!!! I called Tara straight away and she had a letter too!"

I hug Mrs. Clermont, "That is wonderful! I wonder if that agent who visited Eclectic last week did all this? If I ever see him again, I'm going to kiss his face!" Krista has her phone out and is searching the internet for more information. "I found it! I found the article, you guys!"

SCANDAL HITS SMALL BUSINESS COMMUNITY OF FAYETTEVILLE

Breaking news for our local area. An anonymous tip to local law enforcement along with corroborating documents identified repeat real estate scammer, Jonah Peterman (aka Scott Smith) and his attempted real estate scheme that would have been detrimental to the community and commerce of Fayetteville. Peterman, a Nevada native, is wanted in his home state and others, for a complex business scheme to sublease business properties. Peterman has many other aliases such as George Giles, Kent Klent, and Brian Bronsen. Potentially more aliases and possible accomplices may be revealed as this story continues to unfold. Peterman allegedly outbid ending leases to obtain access to business properties. He then posted the properties for illegal sublease as up-and-coming high-end commercial locations. Once obtaining a 1 year's lease payment up front, Peterman absconded leaving the business owners with no true claim to the locations and out thousands of dollars. Peterman has been arrested and is currently in custody with Fayetteville law enforcement without eligibility for bail due to potential flight risk. More to come as this story unfolds.

It's over. Scott is arrested and we get to keep our business. I can't believe it, this is incredible news. My life is falling into place again. Now, I just need to figure out where I stand with Sir. He said he couldn't meet me tonight, so I have some time to think before I talk to him. Krista, Willow, Mrs. Clermont and I go out for dinner and have drinks. When Tara was able to meet us there, we spend the evening sharing fond memories of when we all first opened our shops and the trials you have to overcome as a small business owner.

This is a life that brings me peace and hope for the future, this is the 'new moon' of my life. Someone purchased the lunar series. I need to pack it up for shipment when I get back to the shop tomorrow. I'm going to miss seeing it every day. I sure hope the new owner/owners can appreciate the piece as much as I did.

The next day I receive two certified letters just as I'm leaving the house for work. I can't wait to show Krista because I bet it's our new lease agreement! I'm waving the envelopes in the air triumphantly to Krista when we get out of our cars. We run inside and plop on the little couch in the back office. Excitedly, I rip it open and read the new lease information a loud. We did it!!! Scott is gone and Eclectic is going to be okay!! I won't lose my business or my time spent with my best friend. I sit back against the cushions and sigh, closing my eyes and exhaling all the stress I've been carrying. I hear Krista rattling paper next to me, I assume she is rereading the information. "Hey, Jolie, what's the other letter?"

"I don't know. Let me see." She passes me the envelope. I don't know why it didn't register that the mail carrier gave me two certified letters. "This looks like junk mail, why would it come certified?" I open the outer envelope then pull out another unmarked envelope and then that actual letter.

You've Won!!!! A Very Special Prize!!!!!

Jolie Greenwood   Jonathon Doeinger
Jolie's Eclectic & Vinyl   Sweepstakes Manager
3674 Magnolia Ln St 8   BSBS
Fayetteville, AK 72764   5678 Nouwaire Blvd
                                             Maideuhp, GA 30006

Congratulations Mrs. Greenwood!

You have been randomly selected by the Bureau of Small Business Surveys (BSBS) as this year's recipient of our annual *Glamping in Solitude Sweepstakes*! Every year we draw from regional small business owners to bequeath one very special winner with a once-in-a-lifetime experience camping in luxury. We understand and have the utmost respect for the contribution small business owners provide to the community, this is our way of giving back. Please see the rules listed below to claim your prize. Come relax at our picturesque getaway, secluded in the foothills of the Ozarks. Where you will be surrounded by exquisite views of flora and fauna with all the modern amenities. *We just know you'll fall in love.*

Expectantly,

Jonathon Doeinger

Jonathon Doeinger
Sweepstakes Manager

To claim your prize and remain eligible for receipt please read the following carefully.
- Recipient must respond by registering through the website below within 3 days of receiving this letter.
- NO ACCOMPANYING GUEST
- ABSOLUTELY NONTRANSFERABLE
- Recipient must commit to the full 3-week stay.

Please register for your stay at www.secretemnthideout.com//

The Bureau of Small Business Surveys is a nonprofit organization. No entry fees or kickbacks are allowed for the purpose of this sweepstakes.

Krista is reading over my shoulder. We look up at each other shocked. I've never heard of such a sweepstakes, and I certainly haven't entered any. Krista takes out her phone and does an internet search. In no time, she finds proof this is legit. There are webpages from the nonprofit showcasing other businesses that have won in previous years and pictures of the cabin and surrounding views. It's beautiful. A secluded getaway. "You *have* to go Jolie! This is so awesome! It could be good for the shop, and you totally deserve to have a free vacation after everything you've been through. I can run the shop while you're gone, and I'll take care of BB!"

"I don't know, Krista, with everything that's happened with Scott it might not be a good idea to be away and inaccessible right now."

"Jolie, he is arrested without bail. We don't need to worry about him anymore. I'll still have Willow around too." I look down at the letter, uncertain. "I suppose I could review this website more when I get home and think about it. It says I have three days."

After work, I lay on the couch with BB. She stretches out on her back with her head on my lap, paws up. I have to smile at her. To be so blissfully content is a luxury for sure. She doesn't have to worry about men or leases or bills. I rub her belly and under her chin. I have been looking up the sweepstakes website and the businesses of the past winners. Nothing I found seemed to suggest it was a scam.

The cabin looks incredible, and the surrounding area is awe-inspiring. I could take my camera up there and practice some of my photography skills. It's been so long since I've taken pictures. I wonder if there is even internet out there. Maybe being off the grid for a time would be good for me. I need to evaluate what I am doing with Sir. I suppose I could try meeting him in person, but asking for such a step would surely reveal my true attachment to him. His lack of asking to meet me proves he doesn't feel the same.

I'll let him know tonight that I've won this awesome prize and I'll be away for a while. Having some time away to be with my own thoughts and feelings is exactly what I need. I rub BB's head then move from the couch to the bedroom, scoop up my laptop, and then plop down on my bed. I log onto the website from the sweepstakes letter and have to giggle. The website spells out "secret mountain hideout." That's perfect. I'll hide away and have peace to figure out what path I should take without the distractions of life or the influence of Sir.

Chapter 10
Hello Pet

Jolie

I MISS BB ALREADY. I debated about whether or not to bring her with me. I've never taken her on a trip like this before. I worried about her getting lost while frolicking in the woods. I would never forgive myself if anything happened to BB. Being without her for so long will be super lonely though. I slowly navigate my SUV down the winding path as I make my way to the cabin. I received an email last night with driving directions, this place isn't listed in Google Maps. I'm unsure if that is a pro or con for this trip.

It feels like I've been driving forever when I finally pull up to the cabin. I really am in a secluded mountain hideout. The pictures on the website really did not do it justice. Cabin isn't the right word for this place; it looks more like a mansion. The wood exterior is dark green and matches the a-frame roof. There is a chimney on the side of the cabin that cuts through the roof, the brick is also painted dark green for a seamless exterior design. A stone and landscaped lined path leads up to a porch that wraps around the entire cabin. Rocking chairs with a little side table sit on the left-hand side of the porch and a large porch swing bed hangs on the right. It's dressed with blankets and pillows in moody floral colors. It's almost like this cabin was decorated just for me. I'm in awe.

I haul my bags over my shoulders and waddle up the porch steps to the door. I put the code into the keypad above the doorknob, 43556738#. It seems like an excessive amount of numbers, but as soon as I hit the final # the keypad light turns green, and the lock clicks. I push the heavy door open and continue to be amazed at the luxury of this place. I drop my bags by the door and explore the space. This is so big, seems odd that only one person is allowed to stay. The main living space has a giant fluffy grey rug and big sectional facing the stone fireplace.

There are blankets either draped over every sitting place or a basket with a blanket nearby. The moody color scheme continues around the interior with wallpaper on a few accent walls. I giggle as I pass the hallway, there is a large gold-cast deer head. He's wearing thick-framed glasses and smoking a pipe. I was expecting to see animals mounted all over the walls, but this is much better. I cross to the other side of the cabin to look out the windows at the back of the property. There is a large patio with chairs and a firepit. This place is incredible.

Upstairs there is a reading lounge with floor-to-ceiling bookshelves, more cushy chairs, and blankets. Large windows look out into the forest beyond. The bedroom is definitely my favorite. The bed is gigantic with a heavy comforter in dark green, facing large floor-to-ceiling windows. I bet the stars look so beautiful at night. There is an electric stove that resembles an old-time metal wood stove seated on a stone hearth in the corner of the bedroom. I wish it was winter so I could try it out.

I spent the rest of the afternoon snuggled in the reading lounge; the shelves were stocked with plenty of romance novels. I was surprised a shared property like this would have smutty books, but I am not complaining. Several on the shelf were by my favorite authors. In the kitchen, I found the same brand of herbal tea, coffee, and coffee creamer I drink at home. I even found a container of blueberries in the refrigerator. It's almost spooky how this place seems tailored to my preferences. There are still a few rooms downstairs that I didn't even go in. This place is seriously huge, I'll have to explore more tomorrow.

Maybe I'll go on a nature walk too. As evening comes, I start to feel sad. It's the first night in weeks that I won't talk to Sir. I suddenly miss him so badly that my eyes begin to water. I shake my head to clear my mind and fight back the tears. I know I need to face this. It's the real reason I accepted the prize. Facing the thought of no longer having Sir head-on is immediately devastating. Maybe a long hot shower will help.

It didn't. Even though I tried melting the skin right off my bones I still can't imagine never speaking to Sir again. I wrap myself in the fluffy white bathrobe I found in the closet. My hair sticks to my neck and face, I brush it out angrily. This feels so unfair. Of course, I would meet the man of my dreams, and he wouldn't be real. An online persona. Maybe I'm not meant to find real love. Slamming the brush down, I stomp out of the bathroom, but skid to a stop and scream bloody murder at the man standing in front of the bed. "Hello, pet."

What. The. ABSOLUTE. FUCK!!!!!! It's the real estate agent I met in my shop that day. I stand there with my mouth open in frozen shock as I take him in. He's wearing another suit, tailored perfectly to him. Dark blue with a lighter blue shirt and a grey necktie. The necktie has been loosened a bit at the collar. He stands at the foot of the bed relaxed but confident. His hands are placed casually in his pants pockets. The stubble of his beard calls to me, like before, I'm drawn to rub my face against it. But I'm so confused. Why would he be here? A new company holds the leases to the block and Scott is in jail. Unless he's working with Scott and now he's pissed at me! Maybe he tracked me down to take revenge! My mind is absolutely racing. I can't speak. I can't breathe.

"Speechless, Kitten? I know. Our first true meeting is a momentous occasion; that day at your shop doesn't really count since you didn't know who I was. I'm sure you're quite shocked to see me here. But. You needed me, and so I came to you as any good owner would do for their pet."

I slowly begin to put thoughts together. Shaking my head I ask, "This can't be how, how did you know where to find me? How did you get to the shop that day?" I'm pulling the bathrobe closer to my chest. This is crazy, how did he get into the cabin?

"I knew you were here because this is my cabin, Kitty, I brought you here. You needed a little holiday, it's been so stressful for you. Now, I've let it slide a bit because I know you're surprised to see me, but let's not forget our rule about using honorifics." As if on autopilot I respond, "Yes Sir." He smooths the fabric of his tie down his chest. My eyes follow the path of his hand. Long thick fingers and a broad palm. Short clean fingernails. "What a good girl. I really am so proud of how you've taken to your training so far. I can't wait to see how you blossom under the rest." He claps his hands together in delight. "Now, I've laid out your nightgown.

Get dressed then wait on the bed. I'm going to have a shower and change then you and I will have a talk about my plans for us."

He walks out of the bedroom and down the hall. I tiptoe to the doorway and listen, soon I hear water running from another bedroom. Backing into the room, I shut the door and turn the lock. I could run. I could go right now, run to my car, and get the hell out of here. My keys are on the kitchen counter. I go to grab my phone off the nightstand but stop as I look at the black silk nightgown lying on the bed. I know this is stupid, but I trust him.

Isn't this what I've been dreaming about? That I would randomly meet him one day? That I could have the opportunity to throw myself fully into the dynamic with him, no reservations? Just fully submitting. If he wanted to hurt me, he could have already. I was completely vulnerable in the shower. He didn't come in. He waited until I was dressed to talk to me. He could have handcuffed me to the bed or murdered me already. He wants to talk. Surely, he knows I could run away, but he is giving me the opportunity to make a choice. I think back to all our conversations. How invested in the real me he seemed, not just the sexy-talking me. It's what cemented my deep attachment to him. Obviously, if he didn't also have strong feelings for me the way I do him, he wouldn't have gone to such lengths to bring us together. I slap my hand to my forehead. I am seriously justifying stalking and manipulation tactics.

I slip off the bathrobe and into the nightgown. It's a perfect fit. Next to where it lay on the bed are two little hair clips that look like cat ears. I take them over to the dresser mirror and clip one on each side of my head. A calm comes over me. A feeling of rightness, and contentment. I hear the sound of a door down the hallway and jolt. He said to wait on the bed. I hurry over to sit, then remember I locked the bedroom door. I run quickly to the door, flip the lock, then haul ass back to the bed, plopping on it just in time for him to open the door. Whew, I made it. Pride swells in me. I hope Sir is pleased.

Sir is dressed more casually. His suit has been replaced by lightweight lounge pants and a t-shirt. His hair is damp from his shower, but he didn't shave his face. I lick my bottom lip involuntarily. He stands over by the dresser, giving me as much space from himself in the room as he can. He is so thoughtful, trying to help me feel comfortable in such an unorthodox situation. "You did good, pet."

Sir smiles at me as he leans on the dresser and folds his arms over his chest. I sit perfectly still, waiting for what's to come. Sir has a gentle expression as he gazes back at me. I wonder if he is as surprised as I am that I didn't run. "You look so good with ears on your head, Kitty. I bet you feel better when you're dressed more properly too. Do you have any questions for me before I begin?" I take a deep breath. "Yes Sir, I do. I was wondering if you could explain how you were in my shop that day and how you found me here?"

Sir nods his head, I'm sure he was expecting this question. "I was at the shop, Kitty, because I needed to see all the spaces you occupy. I needed to know everything about you. You see, I've been rather taken with you since our first encounter. By the way, I owe you a punishment for keeping your laptop open and pointed right at your bed. While I've enjoyed being able to watch you all this time, that really isn't safe." I blanch. "You've been watching me, Sir?" Maybe I should have run. Mentally I tally how long I've been talking to him on the dating site and everything he could have seen through my laptop. HE'S BEEN WATCHING ME THROUGH MY COMPUTER. I have a stalker; Sir has been stalking me all this time.

"Yes, Kitty. Always. It was so cute watching you try to be vague about details you thought would help someone find you. You didn't realize what you were giving away or who you were giving it to. I hope this teaches you a lesson about being safe on the internet." Sir goes into detail explaining who he is, his business, and how he found me. As freaked out as I should be, I think of the groceries that kept coming to my house, goodies for BB, the concert...all the things he used his "power" for to make my life easier, better, more enriched. Sir stays on his side of the room. He isn't ogling me; his body language is respectful. I'll admit the sweepstakes thing is a bit more difficult to excuse.

"Wait!" I interrupt him, gaining me a pointed look. "Uh, I mean, excuse me Sir I have another question, please." He nods at me. "That's better, Kitten. Go ahead." I chew my fingernail. "What about the new real estate company that bought the shopping block, Sir?"

He folds his hands together and leans back against the dresser. "Yes, I bought the block. You and your friends won't have to worry about rent increasing or anything else like that interfering with your business. Your speech in the shop that day was very moving; I wanted to give you the freedom to enjoy your shop without any obstacles. And rest assured, that won't be changed or influenced by whatever you decide tonight, Kitten."

"You tipped off the police, Sir?"

"I take your well-being very seriously. Anyone who has wronged you will be dealt with swiftly. Including your shitty ex. I don't care that it was before we met. Rest assured I never fabricated any of their offenses. I merely brought to light things they hid in the dark. Scott and Gary got what was deserved."

I try to keep my breath even to remain calm while I process what he is saying.

"I'm not a blameless man, I have done some very bad things that should send you running for the hills, but I won't apologize. I've watched you without your knowledge, dug through your bank account, and your business files, tracked your phone…I've been in your house, in your shop…I fabricated a surprise getaway to lure you out into the middle of nowhere. All your friends are expecting you to be gone for an extended time, no one will think twice about your absence. I've done all of this for you, my sweet little kitty, because you have been such a very good girl.

My question is, can you live with that? Can you see me for what I am and still wish to be here with me? Stay here with me, in this cabin, for the next three weeks. Let me direct you, train you, and turn you into the perfect kitten I know is hiding deep down inside you. When the time is up, we can go our separate ways if that's what you choose. What do you say Kitten?"

I want to pass out. He must see the trepidation on my face. "I'll give you the night to think on it, pet, we can revisit this in the morning." Sir walks toward me and leans in as if to kiss me, he doesn't though, he looks into my eyes for a moment then leaves the room with a, "Night night, Kitty." I'm left alone. In a cabin in the woods. In the middle of nowhere. With a stalker. A stalker who has broken into my home, played with BB, followed me to work, and bought the building my shop is leased from. He is also a stalker who sabotaged my "enemies"... fed me, played with BB, and healed some of my deepest emotional scars from Gary. A stalker that I am head over heels for.

How does one tuck themselves into bed and rest peacefully while they share a cabin in the woods with their stalker? How does one rationalize the fucked-up draw to a man like this? I can see myself on a daytime TV talk show trying to convince the live audience that I am a fully sane woman who made a fully sane decision.

I'm pacing back and forth in the bedroom. I catch a glimpse of myself in the mirror and stop to really look. The little cat-ear hair clips perch atop my head. I get a hint of that floaty feeling again. I long for the experience of being Sir's pet. To be cared for and used simultaneously. I want to feel cherished, to feel controlled. I must be ***absolutely*** crazy to even consider this. But if I don't. If I walk away, I know the emptiness of being without Sir will be unbearable and I will always wonder '*what if.*' I decided to try and sleep on it even though I know my mind is really made up. Tomorrow morning, I will no longer be Jolie. I will be Sir's pet.

When morning comes, I wash my face and brush my teeth. I adjust the cat ear hair clips and run a brush through my hair. Staring at myself in the mirror I take a few steadying breaths. I am about to go downstairs and tell my stalker to please train me like a pet and have dirty, dirty sex with me for the next three weeks. Yeah, that is a perfectly normal breakfast conversation. I don't bother changing from the nightgown, I like staying in something he chose for me. As I pass the dresser something catches my eye.

There is a small navy-blue jewelry box with a gold bow. There isn't anything to determine the name of the jewelry store but there is a little card slipped beneath the knot of the bow. Penned in neat cursive reads: **Be a good girl, Kitten, and wear these.**   Inside the box is a pair of small gold studs that are in the outlined shape of a cat head. I put them on and look in the dresser mirror. I get the feeling he is going to slowly transform me into the pet of his fantasies. Fulfilling Sir's fantasies excites me, I'm already getting wet at the thought.

When I get downstairs Sir is at the kitchen bar having coffee and typing on his laptop. I bet he is blackmailing someone right now. He looks like he could be reading celebrity news on BuzzFeed but he is probably getting dirt on some government official. I slowly approach the bar keeping the back of the computer to me. I don't want to accidentally see anything that would make me an accomplice. "So, you blackmail people over breakfast and then stalk people in your free time."

He doesn't even look up from the computer. Just grins, "That's not true. I also enjoy woodworking. I made a fair amount of furniture in this cabin. Actually." He takes a sip of his coffee and closes his laptop. "Have you come to a decision, Kitten?"

"Um, yes Sir." I wring my hands in front of me and shift from toe to toe as I muster the courage to verbalize into the universe what I am agreeing to. "I came to tell you that I've thought about your offer, and I would like to try and explore this with you. But afterward, you agree to no more stalking. Sir. After the three weeks, we go our separate ways." I say that last bit with a firm voice and a nod of my head. Even so, the misery that will come at the end creeps at the back of my mind. My neck feels hot and my chest feels tight. "As you wish, pet." He looks a little disappointed. Maybe after sleeping on it, he wishes I would have backed out. Now that he has really seen me in person, maybe he isn't as enthralled with me as he thought while watching me through a computer.

Sir rises from his seat on the bar stool and pulls out the one next to himself for me to sit. He begins making me a cup of coffee just to my preference, of course he knew, and a bowl of Greek yogurt with blueberries and honey. While I eat he goes over the boundaries of our arrangement. We discuss limits, how they can change, when to use a safe word. He is very firm that this arrangement is for both of our pleasure and enrichment, it isn't to be one-sided with him just barking orders and me following like a zombie. He knows I'm a people pleaser at heart and makes me promise not to engage in anything that is a line for me, although this will push me way out of my comfort zone.

When I'm finished, he takes my dishes and cleans up. Gary would have never waited on me like this. I must look confused because Sir explains: "Any good owner would take of their pet's needs, wouldn't they?" I nod along trying to wrap my head around the idea that I am a pet now. A kept person? It's unlike anything I've ever experienced. Sir continues, "and any good owner will correct their pet when mistakes have been made." Oh shit.

"I told you we would have a punishment for you being unsafe with your laptop. You left it open and directed at the bed. A place where you participate in things that make you the most vulnerable...like sleeping, and intimate acts...That won't do, Kitty." He takes my hand and leads me into the living room over to the ottoman. A blanket has been spread out over it. Sir leaves me here and moves to a large wall cabinet. He opens a drawer and pulls out a smooth wooden paddle. "On your knees, Kitty, lean over the ottoman. I laid the blanket out to make it softer for you."

I slowly lower myself down; shit what have I agreed to? I read about spankings, but I've never had one. That paddle looks crazy, it's thick and stubby but it looks smooth. I bet it really pops and Sir holds it like he's a professional spanker. My brain glitches over momentarily from trepidation to extreme jealousy over the idea of him spanking some other sub. "Scoot up Kitty. I want your ass up." I scoot a little further forward. My hips up and my arms dangling over the other side. Sir lifts the nightgown up and bunches it on my lower back. He rubs, squeezes, and slaps at my ass cheeks; he says he is warming me up since it's my first time. How gentlemanly of him. *You will accept correction from your Sir, trusting that he has your best interest in mind and would never cross your limits, but that punishment is not always pleasant.* At the time, I thought this rule was just a formality to cover all the bases. I hadn't thought I'd be living it.

I'm dwelling on this rule when the first real strike comes. I yelp loudly and flail my legs. Sir is chuckling behind me, just great. The strikes continue as does my yelping. "Your safety is very important. I can't have you acting in a way that would put you in risky situations." WACK. "Anyone could be watching you through your laptop, Kitty." WACK.

"Like you, ***Sir***!"

"*Exactly*," WACK. Oh wow, that one really strung. "Now look what's happened. You've been lured away to a secluded cabin for an extended trip. Your friends won't be alarmed by your absence."

WACK. "You're lucky it was me watching Kitty, and not some unhinged psycho." My legs have slipped and I'm sliding backward off the ottoman, I'm gasping to catch my breath. "GET THAT ASS UP." He barks. I scoot back into position as fast as I can. He continues smacking me with the paddle. My ass burns and I know I'm going to be sore for a while. After 10 more strikes, he lets down my nightgown. "Now that we have dealt with that, and I hope you've learned your lesson, we can start to have some *real* fun Kitty."

CHAPTER 11
POP QUIZ

Sir

I'VE KEPT TRACK OF her through my security feed as she arrived at the cabin. The cameras around the house are discreetly placed so anyone who might enter without welcome wouldn't know they were being watched. One is in the eye of a gold-cast deer head that is mounted close to the main entrance. I have them hidden all over the property. There isn't a place she can explore that I can't follow. I watch her drop her bags and walk around the main living room and then up the stairs. She takes a perch in the reading lounge for the afternoon. Unaware that I've arrived at the property, she spends her day engrossed in a new book. I've parked around the back and wait, watching the camera feed from the app on my phone. When she heads to the shower, I grab my bags and go inside.

Seated on the bed in the guestroom just down the hallway from the main, I watch enraptured as she disrobes. Her full breasts jiggle as she wiggles out of her leggings. She brushes her long hair; it looks so silky I can't wait to run my hands through it. I switch camera views to one embedded in the tile work inside the shower. Licking my lips and rubbing my cock through my pants, I watch her nipples harden as she adjusts to the temperature change, the steam rises. I'll have to talk to her about healthy water temperatures. I can tell she's frustrated as she hangs her head under the spray. I know she was coming out here to escape my influence. She thinks I don't care for her, that I could live without her. Soon she'll understand that's not true, I fully intend to keep her, always.

She soaps her hair, arms, and back, her breasts lifting and swaying as she scrubs her scalp. I wonder if she suspects anything. Surely the inkling has started in the back of her mind. She turns her back to the camera and now I get to watch her ass wiggle as she lathers the soap. I'd trade places with that sponge in a heartbeat. She lathers and rubs all over her breasts, arms, and ass. Thoroughly cleaning every spot and my mouth waters with the show. The water turns off and she steps out to get dry. It's showtime. I walk down the hall and lay out the nightgown and accessories I brought her. Taking my position in front of the bed, I wait for my pet to exit the bathroom. Her shock is everything I hoped it would be. I'm enjoying her facial expressions as she does mental gymnastics to figure out why the "real estate agent" is standing in the bedroom. I smile, "Hello, pet."

After some of the shock has worn off, I give her a little "space" and an opportunity to change. Exiting the bedroom, I pull my phone from my pocket and watch as she frets with what to do. She rushes to the door and flips the lock, adorable. I turn on the shower and position the phone on the counter so I can continue to watch her as I get cleaned up and changed. She's dressed now, I can hear her feet pound the floor as she rushes to unlock the door for me and get back in position before I can enter the bedroom. I hesitate at the door momentarily to give her a few extra seconds. When

I finally open the door, my sweet kitten is exactly as I requested. Good, we are off to a promising start.

It's misery keeping up the façade of patience while I fully introduce (reintroduce?) myself to her. She needs the guise of control in this situation, to believe it was her idea to trust me. I gently answer her questions and assuage her apprehensions; modeling a perfect gentleman all while I fantasize about my debaucherous plans. Taking leave to allow her time to make her "choice," I take up my favorite nightly habit, watching my pet sleep. She looks so perfect in my bed, in the nightgown I chose for her, her hair spread out on the pillow behind her. The only thing missing from the scene is me. Soon.

The next morning I'm up at my normal workout time, my internal clock doesn't care that I'm on vacation with my pet. I head downstairs to the kitchen to make coffee and check on the business. Pulling up emails from Lawrence and Davis to respond to; there are potential clients seeking services, but I need to vet them before I accept the work. I click through the emails and send some responses to my crew. Then I check the internet to see how dear old Gary is fairing. I plan to pay him a personal visit very soon. It's late morning when she finally comes down. I keep my face schooled as Kitty descends the stairs. Watching her from my peripheral, I see she found the present I left for her in the bedroom this morning. I stood there for a moment watching her sleep in the morning light, snoring a little, so cute.

I fix my pet some breakfast, one of her favorites. I love the sounds of her munching on the fresh blueberries. I don't know how, but she gets a little yogurt on her nose, I reach over and swipe it off with my finger. I know she lapped up some of the frothed creamer from her coffee when she thought I wasn't looking. Give me time, sweetheart, you won't always be so shy. I see the inner pet hovering just below the surface. I'm going to help you release her. I've learned so much watching her through the laptop camera and eventually following her around town. She has so many little natural mannerisms that are pet-like. A natural submissive, a natural pet. She just needs a good owner to help her realize herself. That would be me.

Once breakfast is cleaned up and we've come to an agreement about the parameters of this "temporary" arrangement, I broach the subject of the laptop. I know it seems unfair to punish her for something I so wholly exploited and benefited from. With that said, she was very lucky it was only me on the other side of that screen. That could have gone very badly for her. Fortunately, I was the one who found her, like a little stray kitten wandering the back alleys, forgotten and left to fend for herself. Now I'm here to take her in, give her a home and help her realize her full purpose.

The spanking I gave her is one she won't soon forget. I had to make a good impression on her. When she started to slip off the ottoman I barked orders to get her ass back up; that was a test to see if she would fight me or take the rest of her punishment willingly. Her submission to me was immediate, I'm so proud of her, not that I really doubted her. Her training so far has come along so nicely. There was a chance she would revolt but her nature up to this point had me confident she would pass my little tease of a test.

Even when she thought I couldn't see her; when she thought I'd never know one way or another; she obeyed every task I ever gave to the letter.

We spend the rest of the morning lounging on the large sectional in the main room. My kitten is draped over my lap while I rub her belly and breasts lazily as we watch some true crime show she wanted to see. I might have to limit her viewing of things like this. It seems intense for a sweet little kitten like her. I scratch her behind the ears, and she smiles. She appears to be content with me here like this. I hold my breath and hope she can learn to be content with me always. This is the life I've dreamed of. Having my pet snuggled to my side; to hold and play with, I have three weeks to convince her this is where she needs to stay. Not locked away of course. She's free to have her own life, to work her shop if she wishes, and pursue all other ambitions, but always with me at her side, watching over her.

She falls asleep like this, her head resting in the crook of my arm, I know she must not have rested well last night with a life-altering choice weighing on her mind. I turn the channel to something about nature and tilt my head back on the couch cushion, eventually dozing off myself, in the blissful contentment of our moment together. It's a few hours later when I feel her stirring in my lap. My arm has long gone numb. I flex my fingers open and close to help regain the feeling in my hand. She sits up and looks over at me. Waiting for direction from Sir, what a good girl, learning already. I brush her hair back trying to smooth it down for her, she leans her head into my hand enjoying the touch. Knowing she's eager for my hands on her is a good sign. I pause for a moment then turn to face her a little more. "Have you been through every room in the house, pet?"

"No, Sir. I've only seen this room, the kitchen, the upstairs reading room, and the bedroom."

"Come on, I have something to show you."

I get up from the couch and reach my hand back waiting for her to take it. I lead her around the hall to the other side of the kitchen, there's another, somewhat smaller living room. As she follows me in, I hear her gasp behind me. "*You* bought it!?" On the opposite wall is the lunar phase art series from her shop. "You said it was your favorite thing in the shop, I wanted you to always be able to enjoy it. I meant it when I said I was inspired by you that day. Your passion for your business community and the artists you help promote in your own shop is inspiring. I want you to be able to have those things to enrich your life for as long as you want them."

She stands there focused on the art. I wonder which of the phases she feels like now. I hope it's still the New Moon, full of hope. She is squeezing my hand, and although it kind of hurts, I don't say anything. I stand in silence with her appreciating the art. The art on the wall, and the art happening between us. I wanted to endear myself to her. I hope I succeeded. My kitty turns to look up at me, her eyes misty with emotion. "Thank you, Sir, you're the best." She whispers it but I hear it like thunder in my ears. I will be the best Sir for her.

In the afternoon I take my kitten for a walk on one of the hiking trails. Her hair is pulled up in two little buns on top of her head with the ear hair clips I gave her. I give her a spray down with bug repellent; when we get back, I'll check her for ticks. I bring out a collar to show her. It's black with a little bell on the front. All the better to hear her as we wander around in the woods. When we exit the cabin, I lift a black leather leash off the hook at the back door and clip the end to the collar. "So, you don't get lost wandering the trails, Kitty." I adjust her backpack with the camera she brought and give her a little kiss on the head. "Are you ready?"

"Yes, Sir." What a good girl, remembering her honorifics. We start up the trail. I give plenty of slack on the leash to allow her to walk comfortably next to me. I enjoy this area behind the cabin and have hiked it many times. I'm glad to see my pet is enjoying the landscape. When things are more permanent between us, we can share this together often. The light filters through the tree branches and casts a magical glow on her face. The reflection of the beams off the bell on her collar sparkles and dances with every step she takes.

The soft jingling of the bell sings a cadence of my pet's movements. I trail a little behind, enjoying the view of her curvy bottom in her hiking shorts. Mostly, my pet is silent. Appreciating the awe-inspiring nature surrounding us. I am able to engage her in some light conversation about our past, how we got to our careers, where our families are, favorite taste in music... I already know all her answers, but it's more meaningful hearing her story told in her own words verses piecing it together through my hacking. I carry the conversation as if I've never heard any of this before. She's so authentic and open. Everything she says or does enthralls me, even down to the way she rubs her itchy nose.

We come around the path and it opens up to an access point of a small waterfall and pool that runs down into a stream. I guide her over to the edge and have her sit on one of the large rocks to take a rest. I pull out the water bottle from my pack and a little collapsable silicone pet dish. After pouring some water into the dish I offer her a drink. She starts to reach for it with her hands, but I pull back. "Nah ah, good kitties lap their water politely." Understanding of the direction takes hold and she leans forward and begins to lap the water with her tongue. Timid at first but as she continues her laps become more natural and fervent. "There's a good girl, here have some of this." I break off pieces of cereal bar and hand feed her. After she's had her snack and a little more water, I bend down to remove her shoes. "Would my pet like to take a little dip in the water?"

"We can get in Sir?"

"Yes, it's not very deep but it's nice to wade in and feel the cool water. The bottom is smooth, so you won't hurt your feet."

After removing our socks and shoes I roll my hiking pants up; leaning down, I undo the button on her shorts and begin to pull them and her underwear down. I also roll the end of her t-shirt up and tuck it into the band of her sports bra.

"I have to take these off, Sir? You aren't taking yours off?"

"I have a special activity planned for you, Kitten, trust me."

We wade out into the pool. I hold her hand tightly to help balance her as she steps over the rocks on the bottom, the water crystal clear and ice cold around our legs. Her gasp at the temperature is so precious. I can see her nipples harden through her t-shirt and she has little goosebumps along her arms and neck. When we reach the center of the pool, I release her hand and give her a moment to look around and splash in the water a bit. "This is really nice Sir, but I don't understand why you have me half naked." Right now, she is bent forward in front of me, hand on her knees, peering through the water. If she had my view she would understand perfectly.

I reach into the cargo pocket of my hiking pants and pull out a wand. I flick it on, and the high-pitched whizz of the vibration catches her attention immediately. When she faces me, the shock of her expression is so adorable I can't help but chuckle. "Hands behind your back, Kitten. This is why you are half-naked in this pool. Have you been practicing your rules? Cuming every night while reciting them?" I already know the answer; I've watched her over and over again.

"Yes, Sir, I have practiced." Her cheeks turn bright red. I plan to make her pussy match that color. I reach down and touch the wand to her clit. She jolts at the sensation, squeezing her arms behind her back even tighter, making her breasts light forward. I pinch her nipples hard with my other hand. The wand is on high, so I know it was a little shock to her pussy. I pull back from her and then repeat the process again a few more times.

"Tell me rule number one, Kitten." I place the wand back on her clit and hold it there.

"You do not cum without permission." She gasps it out. The combination of my torture and the cold water of the pool makes it difficult for her to focus and get out her words. I pull back with the wand. "Very good, Kitten." I give her a second to take a breath then go at her again. "And the next one?"

"Always use honorifics when addressing your Sirrraaaahhhh."

"Excellent, and the third." I bring the wand back to her.

"Aaahhhhccept correction from your Sir with trust. Urrrgghhhhh ah ah ah."

I held the vibration to her a little longer that time. This is intense for her. Being exposed in the woods and the new sensations she's experiencing. Her face has a beautiful flush, and her pussy is blushing pink as she gets closer to orgasm. If she can't hold off, I'll punish her here. I almost hope she fails because the thought of getting her on hands and knees in this pool and spanking her right on the pussy makes me hard as fuck. I reapply the wand.

"The fourth."

"I will remember and will use your safe words when neeeeeddeeddd. Ugh!"

"Do you need it right now, kitten?" I pull the wand away to give her a chance to answer without thinking about trying not to cum.

"No, Sir. I don't need it." She gasps and huffs for air.

"Good. Continue your rules as long as I have the wand on you."

"I will remember to take care of basic needs when Sir is unavailable, such as staying fed and hydraaaaateeeedddd. Gooooooddddd kkkitties know their woooorth and will NOT ahahaaa bully themselves with negative thoughts or acts."

"Very good, Kitten. Cum for me." Her legs are shaking, her head goes back, and she grunts and writhes with the orgasm. I can feel the pulse of her clit kicking against the wand. I put my hand on her shoulder to steady her. Just when it looks like she's coming down she skyrockets back up into a second climax. My kitten is locked in pleasure, her body bent forward now with her forehead on my shoulder, she moans and whines in my ear. Her cum drips down her thighs and the wand, wetting my hand as I continue to hold it to her. One final jolt of her body and I stop my torture. She did so well.

"That's enough for now, Kitten." I kiss her head and rub her back as she tries to catch her breath. "Let's get you back home and all cleaned up. I'm so proud of you, sweetheart." The hike back to the cabin is slower, her legs must feel like jelly. Once we're back, I run her a bubble bath and fix her a sandwich. Blueberries on the side of course. I tuck my pet into bed for the night making sure she is happy and set to rest. I'm trying to slowly introduce her to how things could be, even though it's killing me to hold back. I don't think I can stand another night of leaving her to sleep alone though. No, this will be the last. She needs me by her side. I turn on the app on my phone and lay in bed watching her. I fall asleep watching the steady rise and fall of her chest as she breathes softly into dreamland.

Chapter 12

Owned

Jolie

After our hike yesterday, Sir spent time caring for me, getting me cleaned up, fed, and then put me to bed. The care made me feel equally as cherished as I felt used during our hike. I slept like a baby. Just like yesterday, I don my ears along with the earrings he gave me and head downstairs where he again makes me breakfast. We spent the day together doing what could be described as everyday couple activities. We made homemade pasta for lunch. It was difficult working side by side when he's left-handed and I'm right-handed. Our elbows kept knocking causing flour to go everywhere. Sir just laughed off the mess, no big deal. I wasn't allowed near the stove though. Sir said stoves were too hot for a kitty's paws. Instead, he had me sit on the counter and read him the recipe for the homemade marina.

After lunch, we went for another hike and bird-watching. We saw a Downy Woodpecker. Sir and I followed the sound of it drilling into a tree until we found him high above us. I was able to get a clear shot with my camera. The peacefulness of the forest and the normality of our time together is juxtaposed to the real reason I'm at the cabin. My sex-cation with my stalker. The simplicity and tenderness of these moments seduce me into imagining a permanence to our situation. I shake the thought away. When our three weeks end, he will discard me. He's seen my whole life, how could this fit into it in the long term?

Dusk settled over the forest. We returned to the cabin in silent contentment, moving like a couple who had been together for years. A familiarity that I felt I had not yet earned after just a few days in his presence. Sitting at the kitchen bar, Sir moved efficiently around the kitchen warming up leftovers from our homemade pasta. After dinner, I was instructed to go upstairs for a shower, and he would lay out clothes for me.

I finished my shower and walked into the bedroom. Sir had indeed laid out clothes for me. If you could really call this ensemble clothing; it doesn't look like it will cover anything. Laying on the bed is a see-through candy apple red lace body suit, the headband with cat ears, and a butt plug with a long fuzzy tail attached. I recognize the lingerie and ears, they're from my house. When Gary first left me, I had gone through a phase of extreme retail therapy; I bought all kinds of sexy lingerie, split crotch panties, and toys. I guess I wanted to feel desirable after he discarded me. I never had anyone to wear them for though. Until now.

I had come to terms with the fact that he had been the one sending the groceries and treats for BB; I hadn't let myself imagine him riffling through my underwear drawer, this is an intrusion more intimate. I push the feelings aside because I don't want to face that reality right now. I want to remain safely in the delusion of my stalker as the man of my dreams.

The tail. This is what makes this outfit significant. He keeps adding to my kitten ensemble. First the ears, then a collar and leash, now a tail...that goes in my ass. It's black with a white tip, bushy and soft. I graze my fingers over the fur. I am really doing this all the way. I step into the body suit. It is a split crotch design; the back completely open and tying around the neck. The chest plunges in a deep v all the way to my belly button trimmed in feminine scalloped edges. The lace is so sheer you can see my nipples through it. Not that it would matter. Any sudden movements and the scrape of fabric that covered my breasts would shift to the side leaving them completely revealed.

I adjust the fabric as best I can, trying to cover as much of myself as possible. Next, I don the headband. It's strange how getting dressed for Sir feels. I had somewhat expected to feel embarrassed, exposed, or even demeaned. I don't though. I feel calm, complete even. Caring that he's been riffling in my underwear drawer slips farther and farther from my mind. I want to be his pet, his kitten.

I pick up the butt plug and pet the tail. I love how soft it feels. "Let me help you with that one, Kitten." I turn around to see Sir standing in the doorway, one arm braced on the frame and the other in his pocket. Like he was offering to help me zip up a cocktail dress or clasp a necklace, not insert a butt plug that looks like a cat tail. "Lay across the bed for me, be a good kitten." Like I'm being controlled by an outside force, I turn toward the bed. It is so easy to let him be in control, turn off my brain, and relax into the bliss of obedience. Bending down I run my hands up the soft comforter and glide across the bed until I'm lying face down on the mattress. I feel his hands rub across my exposed ass cheeks, up my back, and back down my ass.

He gives me a firm squeeze, gripping my cheek and lifting it up and apart. He releases me and gives me a hard slap causing me to yelp. Sir chuckles at my response. "You look so beautiful like this, Kitty." I hear the snap of a cap and feel the wet slippery drips on my asshole. He massages the lubricant around my asshole and then pushes his fingertip inside. He is so quiet, methodical even. Then I feel the tip of the plug pressing against me.

I let out a slow breath as he pushes it inside. It stretches me and burns slightly but also feels good. He works it in and out several times, slowly twisting and rotating; playing with my asshole for a few minutes until suddenly he thrust it all the way in causing me to gasp. I had become relaxed for a moment feeling him play with me in a slow lazy manner, now I'm snapped back to reality. I'm lying across Sir's bed dressed as a cat in lingerie. He leans down and kisses the center of my spine. Then leaves the room.

I'm not sure what to do. I'm frozen for a moment as the feel of the plug makes my clit tingle. Do I lay here and wait? Do I follow him? What would a cat do? I decided to get up from the bed and hover in the doorway. I look around until I see him heading down the stairs. I follow slowly until I get to the doorway of the second living room. Sir is sitting in a large wingback chair; he takes a book from the side table and begins to read. He looks over the top of the book at me. It's stern and his eyebrow raises. I think this look means I need to make a good choice. So, I slip down to the floor and crawl on my hands and knees over to the chair. I sit next to him on my knees.

After he's turned a few pages, he reaches over and begins to pet my hair without looking up from his reading. I lean into the touch and rest my head against his knee. It's soothing. Euphoric. Where others would feel demeaned, I don't, instead, I feel special. I stay like this for almost half an hour, sitting in silence next to Sir while he reads. The peace is broken when he stirs next to me. He snaps his book closed and sits in on the end table. "I need to go out for a little while, pet. While I'm out I want you to stay in your bed." He points to the corner of the room where a large fluffy pet bed rests. It's large enough for a grown man to curl up in.

Velvety tufted fabric stretched around a large pillowy cushion makes a cozy nest. Sir remembered my love for moody jewel-tone colors. There's a blanket folded neatly next to it. "Is that my blanket from home, Sir?" I look up at him confused. "Yes, pet. You love to snuggle with it so much I couldn't leave it behind. Your happiness is a priority to me. Do you like your new bed?" I look over at the nest and then back up at Sir. "Yes, Sir. It looks soft and comfy. Thank you for bringing my blanket."

"You're welcome, my Kitten. Remember, I expect you to stay here while I'm out."

"Yes, Sir." I crawl over to the nest and climb inside. It's so soft. The softest thing I've ever laid on. Maybe even better than the bed in the bedroom upstairs. "I won't be long, be a good girl." Sir walks over to me and kisses my head. Then he leaves the cabin without so much as a look back. I snuggle into the nest and pull my blanket over my body. It isn't long before I fall asleep.

I wake slowly; confused about where I am at first. I roll around in the nest and stretch, pushing my hands into the bedding, arching my back and extending my neck. It's such a good stretch that I'm moaning as I tense my muscles. Something in my ass causes me to moan for a new reason. I suddenly remember the plug and realize how wet and sticky I am between my legs. I look up to see Sir standing over me with a gentle smile on his face. As take him in, I notice his hard cock bulging in his pants. "What a pretty kitten

I've found sleeping in her bed. Such a good girl doing as Sir told her and staying put while I was away." He squats down next to the nest and places his hand under my chin. "I have a little surprise for my sweet little kitty. Come on sleepy head." He stands and walks back toward the bedroom.

I climb slowly from the nest and follow him upstairs into the bedroom. I glance at the clock on the nightstand, it's just after 3 am. Where has Sir been all this time? Sir reaches out a hand to help me back up to my feet. He smiles warmly at me and gathers my hair. Now I see what he's holding. It's another black leather collar, different than the one from yesterday, this one has silver letters studded on it, KITTY. He places it around my neck, adjusting the tie of the lingerie so as not to interfere with the collar.

"I picked this out just for you, Kitty. Something special so you will always feel your place." He finishes threading the buckle and kisses my lips so gently, then he takes his index finger and flicks the little black bell in the center. I do feel special. Telling someone they should "know their place" normally is intended to degrade a person, this feels like a declaration, a promise that I will always belong here, under the shelter of Sir's ownership. I let myself fall into the fantasy.

Sir continues to sort some items on the bed. These weren't here when I got dressed earlier but there is the leash from our hiking trip, handcuffs, a bar, and a flogger laid out on the bed. My heart quickens. I'm terrified and excited. "A good pet is obedient to her Sir."

"Yes, Sir."

"A good pet trusts her Sir."

"Yes, Sir."

"What's the safe word, Kitty?"

"Red, Sir."

"Very good Kitty."

He clips the leash to my collar and then the cuffs to my wrist. He wraps the leash around the center of the cuff and then threads it through a loop at the top center of the headboard. Bending me over the end of the bed, he pulls the leash until there is no more slack and my arms are extended toward the headboard, my back arched. Sir rubs his hands down my back and over my bottom. "This is a spreader bar, Kitty, it will keep your feet in place." He proceeds to cuff my ankles to the spreader bar and locks it into place, keeping my feet wide apart. I feel so off-balance and exposed. Dirty. On his way back to standing he takes the opportunity to lick my inner thighs. "Mmmmmm, my pet has been enjoying wearing her tail." He grazes his finger over my clit causing me to gasp. "But I think we can do better."

Next, I hear a whisp through the air then I'm startled by the slap of the flogger to my ass cheeks. It's hard and fast. I gasp, shocked by the sensation, and cling to the leash for dear life. I remind myself of my rules and that part about *trusting that he has your best interest in mind and would never cross your limits.* He isn't being gentle, but I could use the safe word if it's too much. I can take it though. I can be a good pet. After the first few strikes, the sting isn't quite so jarring. It starts to be a welcomed sensation.

It does sting but it's also pleasant. My asshole squeezes around the plug with each strike adding to the pleasure. He strikes me again and again. Taking a pause to rub his hand over my ass cheeks ever so often. I start to cry, not from physical pain. From everything built up in my brain. All the stress from overthinking, feeling unwanted, feeling ugly...it pours out of me in sobs. He purges it from me. Sir stops for a moment, resting his hand on my lower back. "Remember, I won't stop unless you use your safe word."

"Yes, Sir. I remember." I manage to gasp out between sobs. "I don't need it."

Sir continues with the flogger over my ass cheeks and my thighs. The sobs stop and I'm left with this euphoric feeling. I feel all floaty again. The flogging stops. He runs his hands over my backside, admiring the redness he created. Sir leans his body over mine and the pressure of his belt and pants rubs on my sore bottom. The weight of him presses on the plug, I moan. I feel his breath on my neck, my cheek, my ear. "What should I do with such a sweet little kitten?" His hands reach underneath me to squeeze my breasts. He pinches and tugs at my nipples.

"Should I play with her pretty pussy?" He moves one hand from my breast down my belly and to my clit. He circles his fingers around it forcefully and then pinches it. I yelp loudly. "Or should I play with her little tail?" He moves his hand from my clit to the tail, pulling on the plug, tugging and circling it in my asshole. I moan like the kitty he labeled me as when he put this collar on my neck. "Or do I pound her sweet pussy?" He pulls away from me briefly, hands on my hips he wrenches my ass upward. Pulling me back toward him, stretching my arms and arching my back even more.

I hear the jiggle of his belt and the rip of his zipper. Then he enters me roughly, once and then again. I love the way his cock feels inside me. Leaning over my body he wraps his hands over my wrist and lays his full weight over me. He jerks his hips bracing his knees against the edge of the mattress. It's staccato and animalistic.

He grunts and jerks at me. I feel like a used object. A means for his pleasure. I feel dirty. I feel beautiful. I feel alive. "You're such a good little kitty. Letting me fill you with my cock, with my cum."

I moan at his dirty words. "You look so beautiful with your legs spread and your pussy swallowing my cock. My collar on your pretty neck. My pretty kitty."

I'm gasping and having trouble catching my breath as he powers his cock into me. Each thrust grinding the plug in my ass. I feel warmth spreading through my body like I'm on fire.

"My pet. My kitten. MINE!"

The orgasm hits me hard. I scream and wail as my pussy pulses and my legs shake. I sound like a crazy person uttering unintelligible words as I try to agree with all his declarations. It lasts and lasts. I continue moaning and chanting, "Yes, yes, yes."

Finally, he groans out his climax, thrusting hard and deep. He pulls out from me before I'm ready to let him go. I immediately miss his body weight over mine. As I'm panting and trying to come back to my senses, I feel the bed dip in front of me. Sir is climbing on the bed, and he straddles my arms, so his still-hard cock is right in my face. "Be a good kitten and clean up our mess." I stare up at him and open my mouth. Resting my tongue forward on my bottom lip. He pushes his thick cock into my mouth, messy with my juices and his cum. It's salty, tangy, thick. I clean up every drop while he threads his hands into my hair and humps at my face. I relish the moans and hissing from him as I work at my task with enthusiasm.

"Such a good kitten for me. My kitty. My good, good girl," he coos. When I'm done, he slowly pulls away from me and climbs off the bed. I hear shuffling in the room then feel him behind me.

He lifts my tail up and holds my ass cheeks apart, I see a flash. He just took a picture of my pussy dripping with his cum and a tail plugged in my ass!!! "Such a beauty." He praises me. Sir removes the plug gently, then the spreader bar, followed by the handcuffs. He keeps the leash on and leads me to the bathroom.

The leash is fastened to the towel rod. He reaches into the large tub and turns the water on. He doesn't say a word as he removes the lingerie along with his clothes. He tests the water, then taps at my leg and points inside the tub. I step over and stand in the tub. "Hands and knees," he says. I obey without argument. Sir squeezes lavender-scented body wash onto a washcloth shaped like a paw print. He scrubs me down. Washing over my body like it was any other chore. He washes my pussy and asshole, even between my fingers and toes. When he finishes, he throws a towel over me and gives me a rough dry-off.

He lays the towel on the floor next to the tub. "Sit here and wait for me to finish." I climb out of the tub and kneel on the towel. He crosses the room and steps into the shower, he cleans himself quickly, watching me through the glass doors the entire time. Then he dries off and disappears into the bedroom. When Sir returns, he's dressed in black sweatpants, and he is carrying a little tank and shorts pajama set.

It's gray with little pink kittens all over. "Stand up, sweetheart." I do and he dresses me in the pajamas. Sir unclips the leash and leads me back to the bedroom. The comforter has been changed. He pulls the bedding back and guides me to lay down, removes my collar, and then climbs into bed behind me. Sir wraps his arm over my waist and pulls my body flush to his, throwing his leg over mine. He gives me a tight squeeze. "You did so good, Kitty. I'm so proud of you...night night." Then Sir snuggles his face into my neck and falls asleep.

I lay there processing everything I've done since coming to his cabin. Everything that has led to this moment. I imagine the news story playing out about my life and how people watching from their homes while they stuff their faces with microwaved TV dinners will never understand. They'll cover their faces in shock and horror and talk about how stupid I was not to heed all the red flags in this situation. **Headline**: *Independent working woman kidnapped by her stalker and turned into sex pet.*

They'll never understand how I'm feeling at this moment. Instead of misery. Instead of ugly. Worthless. Unlovable. I feel full of love, cared for, and cherished. This crazy man sleeping peacefully behind me and holding me like a child would hold their favorite stuffed animal...humiliated and degraded me...and made me feel the most beautiful and cherished I've ever felt in my entire life. And with that thought, I too drift off to sleep.

CHAPTER 13
SWEET REVENGE

Sir

I T KILLED ME TO leave her alone in the cabin at night, but this had to be done. I have the security system set; if she stays in her bed like a good girl, she is right in the view of one of my cameras. I can check on her obsessively through the night. The drive down the mountain and into the city takes about an hour, if you drive like an absolute maniac like me. I'm fueled by adrenaline and anger. She thinks she hides all those uncertain emotions from me. Her sweet face is like an open book, showing me every single time she feels doubt or "less than."

My tires crunch over gravel as I pull up to the dive bar. A group of motorcycles line the front of the building and a few of the men loiter by the door, smoking. I nod at one of them and he tips his head toward the building, letting me know that the man I'm looking for is still inside. I check on Kitten one more time to reassure myself she is sleeping peacefully then head into the bar. I keep my steps slow and nonchalant. The smell of weed and whiskey greets me as I make my way through the front door. The floor is sticky under my boots; I'm dressed in old jeans and a band t-shirt to blend in with the regular crowd. Taking a seat in the farthest booth where I can still see a good view of the bar top, I slouch down into the shadow and neon lights. Flagging the waitress, I order a burger and a beer to give purpose to my visit.

Lawrence is sitting at the bar, the leather of his cut with this road name stitched on the back. He has his hand clapped down on the shoulder of a very drunk Gary. Poor Gary, his life is in shambles. Now that the sexual harassment scandal has come out full force, he's been fired, can't get anyone in his line of business to give him the time of day, and his new wife left him. Seems she was fine being the other woman when Gary was treating Jolie like garbage, but not when it was her turn. He's been spending his days and nights at this bar racking up quite the tab. One he can't afford now that he is broke, jobless, and soon to be homeless. How will pay for his expensive car? What about the mortgage on his fancy house? The dues to the country club? How will he climb out of this mountain of debt now that he has no cash flow?

Lawrence has been acting as a concerned friend, listening to Gary whine all night about his troubles all the while keeping the drinks steady, alternating whiskey and beer so Gary is completely shit-faced. He'll be so black-out drunk that he won't be able to remember a damn thing about tonight. Finally, when Gary can no longer keep his sorry ass on the bar stool, Lawrence loudly announces that Gary's Uber is here to take him home. He loops Gary's arm over his shoulder and helps him outside right into a nondescript late-model sedan that Davis has idling out front. Lawrence makes his way back to the bar and continues to nurse his beer. I wait 20 minutes, settle my tab and leave.

Davis has been driving Gary around on a leisure ride through the city, giving me time to park and hike my way to Gary's house.

I wait in the shades between where the brick exterior and the fence meet up, slipping my gloves on while waiting for Gary to make it back home. What kind of dumb shit doesn't have a home security system, cameras, or at the very least motion sensory lights? Nothing, he has nothing. What he has is a bogus sign in the front yard so people think he has a security system. Figures. Men like Gary think they can get through life on false bravado, ass kissing, and manipulation.

My patience is spent, it's getting late, and I want to get back to Jolie. If she wakes up seeing how late it is and I'm not there...hopefully our hike today wore her out enough that she'll sleep right through until I get back. I wait until I hear the approach of a car, watching the headlights slowly turn the corner and come up to the house. I hear Gary's drunken rambling about some bitch being the cause of all his troubles. He can barely make it up the walkway to the front door. After wobbling around for a bit, he opts to go around to the garage and try to enter there. Even better for me.

Dumbass can't get the key in the lock though. I slip around the back, of course, the gate is unsecured. I roll my eyes. Thankfully Jolie isn't still with this bastard; I don't want to think about her living here with no safeguards. Annnnddd keeping on theme, the sliding door from the back patio is also unlocked. Gary, you fuck-up, if you weren't so drunk you could have just walked out back to get into your house. Instead, I'm making my way through the home to the garage entrance to let Gary in.

I flip the lock and crack it open, stepping back so he doesn't see me. I don't want to chance that he has any memory that someone else was in the home this evening. Gary literally has to crawl through the door. I kick it closed with my boot. He lays passed out on the floor. I nudge him a few times with no response except some murmuring about feeling like he wants to vomit. If you want to throw up now Gary, just wait until the morning. I lift the gas can that I carried in with me and head upstairs. The first thing I douse is the bed; I wonder if this used to be his and Jolie's bed? The thought of him touching her spurs me on in my efforts, sloshing gasoline over curtains, on furniture, in closets. I continue down the stairs, soaking every room.

Once I'm satisfied, I head back toward Gary. I use my boot to flip him over and shake the can a little to sprinkle gas on his shirt and shoes, mimicking splash back as if he had doused the house himself. I lean over, grab him by the collar, and haul him up. He fumbles around as he blindly walks straight ahead. Still completely shit-faced, I stick another beer I loaded up with whiskey in his hand. He starts chugging and makes his way out into the lawn. I follow him outside. I had already checked the neighboring houses for any camera feeds that might pick up what was happening over here. They are playing on a delightful loop of a quiet night in the neighborhood.

Once we are far enough away from the house, I stick my boot out and trip Gary. He falls face first on the sidewalk, blood runs down his face, he groans and rolls to his back. I take the beer out of his hand and nudge the handle of the gas can to his palm, he grips the handle, and I pour a little more beer into his mouth. Fucker leans up and tries to drink, gulping down what doesn't pour out onto his chest. What a nice little picture I've painted for the police in the morning. Bastard down on his luck, burns down his own home. Gary lays his head back down and passes out. I lean over him and scape a match across his face, grazing through his stubble hard enough to light. I flick it at the front door and watch as the flames race through the home.

Whistling, I walk at a leisurely pace back to my car. I've ended the fake feed to the neighboring houses. It won't be long before someone calls the fire department, but I'll be long gone before they get here. When I get back to my car I strip out of my clothes and throw them in double trash bags. Once I've changed, I drive along the highway until I reach an old, dilapidated warehouse with a construction dumpster outside. I discard my bagged clothing there and continue on my way back to the cabin. It's really late, I'm exhausted but also charged. My sweet kitten rests peacefully inside, none the wiser to what I've been up to tonight. If she asks I won't lie. I'll never lie to her. What I will do, is take out anything and everything that has ever caused her hurt. Past or present.

Tension rolls through my body as the shower spray pummels against my skin. I scrub the remnants of tonight from my skin as I try to tame the adrenaline still pumping in my veins. I know exactly what I need to find relief. A claim. I need to take control of my sweet little kitten and let her know exactly how much I care. I turn off the water, throw on some clothes, and head down the hallway. Opening the trunk, I pull out a selection of items and then return to the bedroom. It's late, I should let her sleep, but I need her. I can't resist.

I slowly descend the stairs and into the living room where I left her all those hours ago. She breathes slowly, deeply, as she continues to sleep. I stand there, awe-struck, watching. Enamored by her perfection. It's like a dream standing here with her right before me, dressed up in her ears and tail, feeling so content in the pet bed I gave her that she would sleep the night away. Sensing my presence she stirs and stretches.

A good hard play was exactly what I needed after tonight's work, I clean my sweet kitty up and get her into bed. Exhaling into her hair, I fall asleep with her pulled tightly into my side. I worried that she might balk at my sleeping in the bed with her, but the rightness of it has me making a mental declaration to never sleep separated from her again.

We sleep in until late morning. I can't believe I did that. I guess I was out all night, but even then, I should have woken early as usual. Rolling to my side I feel her warmth and pull her close. She snuggles into me like this isn't the first time we are waking up together. What's between us is natural, emanate, unyielding. My cock throbs as I rock my hips against hers, I run my nose down the length of her neck lapping at the curve where her neck meets her shoulder. She moans and wiggles against me. "Did you sleep well, Kitty?" My voice comes out gruff and deep.

She turns her face into mine and kisses the corner of my mouth gently. "Yes, Sir, you've worn me out though, what time is it?' I lift my head over hers to see the clock on the nightstand. It's 10:30 a.m. Fuck, I did sleep in. "It's mid-morning Kitty. How about I go downstairs and fix us some brunch? You can linger here until it's ready if you'd like a few more minutes to rest." She stretches beside me. I love the way she arches her back and grunts into the stretch, lifting her breasts as her arms extend over her head.

I can't help but lean down and take a nip at her then suck one of her nipples through the fabric of her pajamas. She giggles and she tries to wiggle away from me, but I have her locked in my arms, nowhere for a kitty to escape. Grinding my cock down into her while I devour her mouth, and neck, and lick up the side of her cheek. She moans and giggles at my attacks. Finally, I lay a giant smacking kiss on her lips then swat her ass before vaulting off the bed.

Downstairs, I start pulling fruit from the refrigerator and fix her a cup of coffee. Taking a skillet out, I get started on an omelet. Just as I'm finishing up, my kitten is slowly meandering into the kitchen. "Have a seat at the bar and I'll bring you a plate. I've made us omelets and fruit, and your coffee is already there." I nod toward her usual perch. She gets settled and we both dig in. "You'll have me spoiled if you keep up all this cooking for me, Sir." I smile back at her. "Maybe that's my evil plan, have you so spoiled that you can't live without me." The sounds she is making as she eats are killing me. The omelet might as well be giving her a dick down with the way she is moaning. "I did good on the meal then?" She blushes and smiles as she takes her final bite. "Yes, that was delicious. You are an excellent cook, everything you make is so good." I smile wolfishly at her, "I can think of something I'd rather eat."

The blush that hits her face is priceless. I rise from my stool to collect dishes and lean in to kiss her neck as I pass by. I return and coax her off of her stool. I turn her around and sit her up on the countertop. Caging her in with my arms. "I know you love blueberries, Kitty, but do you know my favorite fruit?" She blinks back at me, trying to think of all the things she has seen me eating here at the cabin. "No, Sir, I don't think I do." Hmmm, I hum into her neck as I reach behind her to the fruit bowl and pluck up the ripe round fruit, bringing it into her view. "It's peaches, Kitty, I love to eat peaches."

I back away and pull a knife from the block, cutting the peach in half, juice runs down my forearm. I cut out the pit and place the knife in the sink. I hand half the peach to her as I take a hulking bite out of mine causing juice to run down my chin and onto my bare chest. She stares back at me gingerly holding her half. "I have a task for you, Kitty. I want to help you enjoy that peach you're holding."

I bite into my half, holding it with my teeth while I step forward, grab her pajama bottoms, and tug them off. I toss them aside and lift her heels so they are perched on the edge of the countertop, opening her up wide for me. Thrown off balance, she places one hand behind herself the other holding the peach above her belly. I slurp as I take another bite out of my fruit. "Hmmm the juice is so good, makes my mouth water." I'm staring right at her pussy as I say it. "Take your peach, Kitty, I want you to rub it all over your pussy." I love making her perform for me. Making my sweet wholesome Kitty turn into a very dirty girl.

She turns the peach over, so the juicy flesh is facing her skin and begins to rub up and down over her pussy. I reach forward, placing my hand over hers, grinding the fruit down into her, and rubbing it in circles over her clit. The juice squeezes out and the debaucherous sounds of wet squelching echo in the kitchen. Juice is dripping off the edge of the counter and onto the floor. I keep taking giant bites out of my side of the fruit until it's gone.

"Hmmm, delicious, but that wasn't enough. I'm still hungry, Kitty." I lean in toward her center, lick upward to her clit and take a big bite out of her peach. I keep my face in place as I chew, letting the drop of my chin grind into her swollen clit. I slurp the juice from her center then take my hand and continue grinding the fruit into her, making even more juice run down over her pussy and thighs. It's a big mess, but I'm going to clean it all up. "Cum for me Kitty, show me how sweet that peach can be." I grind harder on her clit, juice and fruit squishing out all over her. She cums, her legs shaking, eyes locked on mine. I lift the demolished fruit and shove it in her mouth, letting the juice and bits of the fruit's flesh roll down her chin and neck. The sticky liquid seeping into the top of her pajamas.

Keeping my eyes locked on hers, I hook my hands underneath her knees and lift her legs. Tipping her back, she is balanced on her ass and holding herself with her hands behind her on the counter. I lower my face to her pussy and run my tongue over the lips and the creases of her thighs, cleaning the sticky sweetness from her skin.

I fix my mouth over her clit and suck hard, then drag my teeth over her. She's sensitive from already cumming and her gasping yelps muffled by the fruit in her mouth have my cock hard and straining. I eat, and eat, and eat, the mix of her tangy cum and the sweetness of the peach driving me out of my mind. When she climaxes again, I drive my fingers inside and press hard against her anterior wall, prolonging her orgasm and sending an extra flood of cum to drip down to the crack of her ass.

I grab her upper thighs and jerk her hips forward, then band one of my arms behind her back. She latches onto me with her arms and legs. "Mmm what a sweet peach," I growl out. I pull down my sweatpants and line up the head of my cock. I lean forward and bite the other side of the peach she still holds in her mouth while I thrust myself inside.

I keep my mouth locked on the fruit, squeezing even more juice out into her mouth and down her throat while I lift her up and then bury myself deeper inside. Her nostrils flare as she breathes heavily through her nose trying to swallow the juice running down her throat. I rut into her roughly, digging my fingers into her soft flesh. Grinding into her like a madman, both of us grunting and moaning gagged by the fruit. When she cries out another orgasm, I let myself go, pumping hot jets of cum inside her sweet pussy.

I pull away, taking the peach out of her mouth. It's just a pulpy mess at this point. "That's why it's my favorite, Kitty." I lick a drip of juice from the tip of her nose then kiss her deeply. "You're a mess, Kitty, let's get you cleaned up." I cup my hands underneath her ass and lift her from the counter. She drapes herself over my shoulder, exhausted. As I carry her upstairs she feels like home to me. "I think after a shower let's go back to bed huh, Kitty, we both had a long night." She murmurs something I can't understand but I take it as a yes.

Chapter 14
Who's a Good Girl?

Jolie

I FEEL LIKE I'M suffocating. I'm sweating and my face is smashed into a blanket or pillow? I'm not sure. As I begin to rouse more fully, I realize I'm being suffocated by a large beast of a man who is laying across my body. As I stir, he squeezes me tighter. Pressing his hips into mine and bringing me impossibly closer to his chest. I was wrong; he isn't a beast, he's a boa constrictor. At this rate I'm going to have broken ribs; I wiggle until my head extends to find tender flesh and I nip at his neck.

I immediately receive a hard slap to my ass. "Bad kitty." He grunts at me. "Keep that up and you'll end up leashed for the afternoon." I hope he can't see my blush at the mention of the leash. He leans down and kisses me deeply, holding my hair at the base of my skull and tightening his other arm around my back again. When he backs off, I can finally breathe deeply. He squeezes my ass and rolls himself out of the bed, stalking into the bathroom. When he returns, he's holding my ears and the collar. Sir leans over the bed and fixes them on me. "There, that's so much better isn't it." Not a question but a declaration. The days are blurring together. Each morning starts the same. I've fallen into this dream world with him, far removed from reality.

Today he dressed me in a silk camisole and crotchless black lace panties so I can wear my tail. He comes up behind me in the bathroom mirror, my eyeliner in hand. Wordlessly he begins to write "Naughty Kitty" across my chest where the camisole v's. "There, now every time you pass a mirror today, you can be reminded not to bite me." He grins then kisses my cheek and gives my breast a tight squeeze. After my breakfast, we lay together on the couch. Sir pets my hair as he reads and we enjoy the peace of the morning. After about an hour has passed he puts down his book. "As much as I'd like to lay here on the couch with you all day, Kitty, I need to check in on work. I'll be in my study for a while, but I have something that I think would keep a mischievous kitten entertained in my absence."

I sit up from his lap as he reaches into the drawer of the end table and retrieves what looks like a small racket ball. I feel a little confused, he wants me to play with this bouncy ball? He's laughing softly, "I know it isn't made of yarn sweetheart, but I think you'll enjoy it for the time I need to take care of some business. Now stay here in the main living room, I'll know if you venture off." He reaches forward and jingles the little bell on my collar.

"Yes, Sir. I'll be good."

I'm sitting on the floor in the hallway bouncing and catching the little ball. I keep watching the clock that sits on the end table; it's only been 45 minutes since he left to check work emails, but it feels like an eternity. When did I get so addicted to his attention and physical presence...? Oh I know, the moment we met. I bounce it a little harder, pouting at my solitude. I bounce it even harder this time and miss the catch; the ball travels toward the dining room, hitting the side of the dining chair, and ricocheting to the wall. This makes the ball gain momentum heading back toward the dining table.

I'm frantically racing back and forth snatching at air to catch it, my bell jingling erratically. What if I break something? Sir will be so upset. The ball bounces on top of the table and into the glass bowl of the pendant light that hangs above, fuck! The light starts swinging back and forth from the impact like a pendulum. Double fuck. I climb into a chair and then carefully onto the table. I'll probably break this table standing on it, but it feels pretty solid as I slowly rise up and stick my hand into the glass bowl to retrieve the ball and stop the light from swinging around.

"Well, well, it seems I have a kitty who enjoys climbing on furniture."

Triple fuck, he did say he would know if I left the living room. I turn around to see Sir standing in front of the table, his classic 'hands in pockets' stance. I launch into apologetics, not sure if I'll be in trouble for being in the dining room or being on this nice table, maybe both. "I'm sorry, I'll get down right now. The ball bounced into the light fixture. I don't think I messed up the table though."

"How would you have messed up the table, Kitty?" His brow furrows and his smile fades. "Um...well... because I'm not a...a super small woman... so ...I really shouldn't be climbing on furniture." I hop down from the chair with both my hands clasped around my little ball. "I see," he says. "It would seem that no matter your extensive practice, you still have not committed your most basic rules to heart." Oh, no. "What do you mean? I memorized all of them. Didn't I prove that on the hike, Sir?" He sighs and fingers a strand of my hair gently. "You proved you could say them while under distraction, Kitty, but you have not yet internalized them I'm afraid. They aren't just something I want you to be able to parrot. Think: surely there is one that stands out to you now?" I mentally run through all my rules trying to find one that applies here and when I get to the last one, I gulp. "Good kitties know their worth, Sir."

"Come along Kitty, let's deal with this right away." I follow him into the main living room with my head down and dragging my feet. I bet I'm about to get my ass paddled. I start trying to reason with him. "I wasn't really putting myself down, I was just being logical that the table wasn't made to hold me, and I shouldn't have been up there, Sir. People aren't meant to climb on furniture." He doesn't respond so I continue. "I would never have gotten on the table if the ball hadn't accidentally bounced into the light." Still nothing. He moves a large wing-back armchair into the center of the room facing the fireplace.

"You aren't regular "people" are you though? You are my pet. And you would be on that table if I directed you to be there, Kitty. I made that table myself, and I have high expectations of what can be accomplished there. Now let's get to the business of correcting your behavior in regard to breaking one of your core rules...don't look so terrified, this will be quite manageable for you." He smirks as he sits down in the chair. "In fact, I've been waiting for an opportunity to use this. Go and stand over there." He steeples his fingers and nods toward the fireplace. "I'm going to put on some music, and you will dance for me, Kitty. Entertain me with the beautiful curves you seem to underestimate."

My brain pulls up the scene from "True Lies" where Jamie Lee Curtis has to do that sexy dance... I bet he is gonna put on something super sensual and slow. The mortification rises in my chest. He flips through his phone with a shit-eating grin, and I just *know* I am about to be completely and utterly embarrassed. All the times Gary told me I wasn't sexy or made me feel awkward and uncool come flooding back, like when I tried that striptease workout video, and he straight up laughed at my efforts...

"Kitty..." My eyes snap to his. "...make sure that tail is swishing."

The overhead surround sound speaker starts to thump with a familiar base intro....... it's "Baby Got Back!!!!" Fuck, he said he watched me through the laptop camera. How many times did he watch me do my version of rump shaking to songs like this while I did housework? He is staring at me, expecting the same unfettered energy I gave when I thought no one was watching...I'm screwed. Sir Mix A Lot is professing his love of voluptuous ba-donk-a-donks while my Sir looks on with a wolfish gaze. He's sitting back in the chair like he is relaxing for a long performance, his chin resting on his knuckles.

I take a deep breath, listen for the beat, and jump myself around so I'm facing backward to Sir, brace my hands on my knees, and start shaking my ass. I wiggle my hips and try to swish the cat tail around like a helicopter. Jumping back around to the front, I gyrate, shimmy, and sway like my life depends on it. It's actually kinda fun and Sir seems to be enjoying himself. I feel absolutely ridiculous though, giggling as I continue the dorkiest dance routine I can muster. The song ends and I'm out of breath. Sir stands and applauds my efforts with a slow clap. "That was wonderful,

Kitty. You have a real talent for dance. Now, let's dispel this notion that you can't be on the table."

He takes my hand and guides me back into the dining room. Pulling out a chair he has me step up onto the table. I'm standing in front of him, it feels a little scary being up here like this. Sir takes his index finger and runs it through my labia. He really is getting his use out of having me in split crotch undies all the time. "Hands behind your back, Kitty." I slip my arms behind my back and lock my fingers around the opposite forearm. Sir leans forward and begins to lick at my clit. "Step out farther, Kitty." With more space between my legs, he is able to run two fingers back and forth over me until he finally slips them inside.

His other hand is wrapped around my hips with his fingers squeezing my ass cheek. He licks and sucks at me while his fingers move in a scissoring motion inside; he twists them around while he continues eating me out. "Go ahead and cum when you're ready, Kitty." I didn't realize that I had been automatically holding back, waiting for his permission. I guess he really is training me. Another minute of his attention and I'm calling out, legs shaking and digging my fingers into my own skin as I try not to let my knees buckle. "That's better." He removes his fingers from me and sucks them clean.

The days pass this way. Sir dressing me, feeding me, grooming me. The outfits become more and more "kitten" as the days go on. I've gone from just the ear hair clips to a full get-up with ears, tail, collar, (sometimes the leash) and these little mittens that have rubber paw pads on them. He got a really good laugh out of watching me try to fix my headband while wearing the mittens. I bumped my head on the end of the couch while crawling around and knocked the headband sideways. I had to literally paw at my head to straighten it. He has been feeding me bites of food by hand or laying it on a small cheese board for me to eat while on my hands and knees.

Instead of a drinking glass, he has been offering me a small dish to drink from. Maybe I'm losing my mind; each day it's easier to descend into the mental space that I am a pet. A kept kitten. It has become too natural to stay on my hands and knees moving around the cabin, rubbing my face against his knee while I sit at his feet, against his face while I sit in his lap.

I've lost track of time, I've lost track of the days. Nothing matters but my interactions with Sir. No outside world interferences. His care. His tenderness. His roughness. His rules. His ownership. That is all that concerns me now. Just existing here with him. Is it morning? Evening? What day of the week is it? I've been resting in my nest, reading a book while Sir was working in his office again. "Hello there, Kitty, are you being a good girl?" I smile up at him adoringly. "Follow me, sweetheart, I have a treat for you." He starts walking toward the kitchen and I follow on my hands and knees after him, looking up at him the whole way we go. My crawling is accompanied by the rhythmic jingle of my collar. It's playful tinkling, guiding me deeper and deeper into my submissive state.

He stops at the kitchen counter and when he turns around, I see he's holding a dainty China tea saucer. It's a beautiful Royal Albert Old Country Roses design. The saucer's edges are ruffled and gilded. "A beautiful kitten deserves her treats on a beautiful saucer, I think." It holds a small mound of fresh blueberries; I can't help but lick my lips excitedly at the sight of them. "Oh, you would like to earn some blueberries Kitty?" he asks. I nod my head vigorously, rising on my knees to paw at his thighs. "Then sit back on your bottom." I obey immediately and am rewarded with a blueberry popped into my mouth. I smack my lips and chew loudly, enjoying the sweet burst in my mouth. Sir pets down my head and scratches behind my ears, careful not to disturb my ear headband.

"Ready to follow some commands, sweetheart? Spread your thighs as wide as you can, Kitty." I slide my knees over the tile floor, opening my thighs as far apart as I can, exposing my pussy to him. "Oh, yes. That's a very good girl. Now rub your clit slowly, sweetheart. Yes, that's perfect." I use the soft rubber paw pad of my sock to slowly rub circles around my clit, I can feel the wetness soaking through the cotton of the sock on my hand. I lick my lips, eyeing the blueberry dish. He pops another blueberry in my mouth, I gobble it greedily. "My kitty loves blueberries, doesn't she? Aren't they sweet and juicy just like you are, Kitty, and so good for you too, sweetheart? But you have to earn them by being a good girl, isn't that right?"

"Keep rubbing, sweetheart." I can feel my pussy getting all sticky as the squelchy sounds are getting louder. I'm staring lazily at the dish of blueberries as Sir plucks the last berry, a fat juicy one, from the now empty dish. I track his fingers as they approach my lips. He starts to place the blueberry in my mouth then tells me, "Hold out your tongue and balance the berry, Kitty, don't eat it or let it fall." I hold my tongue out past my lips to balance the blueberry carefully. My eyes cross as I try to concentrate fully on my task and maintain the circular motion on my clit. The cool feel of the tile floor under my butt cheeks is getting slippery as I get wetter and wetter, and it's difficult to sit perfectly still.

The drool is overflowing the sides of my mouth and trickling down my chin and throat. "You are so beautiful posed like this Kitty." Sir reaches forward and jingles the little bell on my collar. Next, I feel the smooth, warm skin of his cock graze the side of my cheek on the right and left, collecting the drool that's poured over there. He rubs the sides and tip of my tongue, careful not to jostle the blueberry I'm still balancing. "What a talented girl to balance that blueberry so well. You may eat it now, Kitty."

I quickly gobble this one up and look up to his face eagerly for my next trick to earn another, only he isn't holding the saucer anymore. Sir has exchanged the dish for the matching teacup. The moody floral color scheme and its gilded rim are enveloped in his thick, rough fingers as he carefully brings it close to my lips. I can smell the fresh milk as the teacup gets closer to my face. "Have some licks Kitty girl, I know you must be thirsty after all those blueberries." I immediately begin to lap up tiny flicks of the milk, my face getting closer and closer to the cup until I almost plant my nose right into the cool liquid. "Ah, greedy girl." He bops me on top of the head and pulls the cup away from my mouth.

Milk dribbles all around my mouth and down my chin and my tongue continues to lap out to clean as many drips as I can catch. "Does my greedy girl want more milk? Or, perhaps you'd like to earn some cream." Sir brings his cock to my mouth, brushing the head along my bottom lip. I quickly move to lap at the head in long, indulgent strokes of my tongue. He slides fully into my mouth, slowly pulling out and back in again, pulling moans and hums from me as I slurp around his fat cock.

Sir's left hand is in my hair massaging the back of my head lovingly while he whispers soft encouraging praises to me. I'm gulping him down at this point, grunting in pleasure, my paw is soaked where I continue to rub myself. "Keep going, Kitty, but don't cum." I grunt again, this time in frustration. I just want to fall over the edge into oblivion; I'm so consumed in the moment with him, it's hard to hold on and keep control of myself. Sir begins to thrust hard toward the back of my throat, the stimulation to gag causes me to clench around the anal plug holding my tail in place, the added sensation to my ass heightening the already consuming pleasure I'm experiencing.

Sir bends down on his knees in front of me, his hand still behind my head to guide me down with him, my mouth never leaving his cock. My left hand comes forward to help me lean down to the floor, my right still rubbing my clit. My knees are spread as far apart as I physically can get and I'm slipping on the floor in my own wet juices.

As I continue to gasp and grunt while I suck Sir's cock, he abruptly pulls out from my mouth earning a disgruntled mew from me. His grip on the hair at the back of my head is unyielding as he pulls my head back, "One more trick for me, Kitty, hold out that pretty pink tongue for me." His hand slips from behind my head to grip my chin and hold my face steady. "Don't worry, good kitties always get their cream," he grunts as he pumps every drop onto my tongue. He puts both hands into my hair to hold it away from my face so as not to block his view of me. "There you are sweetheart, you've earned yourself such a treat." I hold my head as steady as I can, the salty cream dribbling down the corners of my mouth as it mixes with my saliva, my right paw continues on my clit. "Cum Kitty, cum for me like a good little pet." And I do, I explode as I continue to hold his cum on my tongue.

I am absolutely feral. Grunting and moaning, open-mouthed, eyes locked on his. The cup and saucer clatter on the tile as my knees slip and slide on the now slick floor, writhing in my pleasure. "Whoa, easy Kitty girl, you'll break your pretty dish." He cups my chin, bringing my lips together, allowing me to swallow. His strong arms wrap around my body, pulling me into his shoulder.

I continue to writhe and cum as my body shakes and I hump my paw over and over, gleaning every ounce of this orgasm as I gasp and grunt against his shoulder. Sir reaches around behind me and pulls gently on my tail; he wraps the tail around his fingers, causing the plug to twist around in my ass. Then he gently starts to tug the tail in a little peppered rhythm, causing me to rocket right back up into climax. I cry out in what is an almost painful ecstasy, my back bowing up as I convulse through it. "Mmmmm, its fucking delicious to watch you fall into the abyss of pleasure like that, Kitty. You've made me so proud, sweetheart. But you are such a mess, let's get you all cleaned up and have a cuddle."

Chapter 15
I Fucked Up

Sir

I'M LULLED INTO THE contentment of our easy routine. It feels so natural, I am blissfully happy. Kitty. She's perfect. I make her breakfast, put on her collar and tail, then we spend quiet time together. Connecting physically. Petting, grooming, playing. She is usually ready for a nap in her nest about midafternoon. I work while she sleeps. It warms my heart to look over and see her snuggled in her blanket pile sleeping peacefully, knowing she can trust that I'm taking care of her. We are coming to the close of our three week hiatus. I rub away the physical ache in my chest I feel when I entertain the thought that she may reject this dynamic when we return to the "real world."

I can't let her go. I mean, I won't hold her here against her will, but I can never leave her. I'll always be watching. It won't matter if she ditches the laptop and moves to Antarctica. She could be hiding in a snow cave with polar bears and penguins, I will still find her. I tried to be as honest with her as possible about who I am. I don't want her to feel surprised by my life or have any hidden secrets between us. She needs to go into this with her eyes wide open. I smile as I think about her chasing me through the cabin as I flicked the feathered end of the cat wand back and forth. She was reluctant to chase it at first, but a swift pop to the ass with the wand changed that in a hurry. The sound of her little bell jingling erratically and how her fury at me morphed into laughter rising through the cabin filled me with such joy. A lightness that was missing for me before she came into my life.

I put my work computer away. Peterman still seems to be "comfortably" set up in jail. Making sure he won't come after Kitty is imperative. I had maintained surveillance of the pawn shop after the sale of the laptop; I need to make sure no other accomplices are coming back for it. At least Frank only keeps paper records of sales. Davis was able to break in and obtain it, now shredded and burned. If anyone comes to the pawn shop looking, they won't find information on Jolie. Davis has been keeping an eye on Eclectic & Vinyl and Krista's neighborhood. He jogs the block while she walks BB in the evenings. Just in case. I need to make sure all of my kitten's favorite things are taken care of.

Gary has been arrested for arson and insurance fraud. I smile at the updated news article. There is a particular joy that comes from watching one's enemy's demise. I'm feeling rather accomplished. This brings me back to my early days and doing favors for "businessmen." Now those men owe me some favors, and I intend to cash in once Jonah Peterman is formally sentenced.

Kitty stirs in her nest. I check my watch and smile. She is a creature of habit, her naps usually last about two hours. Then she needs a slow lazy wake-up with snuggles and rubs. I am more than happy to oblige her. Kitty climbs onto the couch and slips between my lap and the laptop, nudging it with her head until I lift it up to make room for her. She twists her body back upright, hooking her arm around my neck and then straddling me, wrapping both arms over my shoulders. I pass the laptop over to the end table and then run my hands through her hair as she rubs her face against my short beard. I could stay in this bliss forever. She sighs contently and relaxes her body forward against me. I run my hands down her back, over her ass cheeks, and fluff her tail. I slide my hand from underneath and cup around the base of the tail where it's plugged in her asshole and then run my hand up the length of it slow and rhythmically.

She moans softly in my ear, basking in the simple pleasure of our touches. "Do you like this tail, Kitty?" I whisper the question in her ear as I continue rubbing her ass and fluffing the tail. She moans a drowsy "mmhmm" from my shoulder. "What if I said I had a new tail for you? One for special occasions." She lifts her head to face me, eyes bright with intrigue. I've noticed that when she is deep in the kitten headspace she talks less and less, using facial expression and body language for most of her communication. "Come upstairs, let's see how complete a kitty I can make you," I murmur the words to her as I place my forehead and nose on her own. I hope she understands the emotional undertones of what I've said.

She follows silently, hovering in the doorway of the bedroom. I call to her with a clicking of my tongue and open hand to coax her all the way in. Kitty slinks to her hands and knees, cautiously making her way over the bed. I continue to click and pat the mattress to coax her all the way up onto the bed. Sweet girl, sitting on her knees so properly, hands on her thighs, looking down at the items I have laid out. One of the best ideas I ever had was making sure to keep her in crotchless panties at all times. I graze my fingers up her thigh slowly then softly brush over her clit earning me a soft mew. Her eyes are on me now, instead of the bed.

"I made you something special Kitty." I nip at her earlobe and kiss her temple. Continuing my gentle brushes of her clit, I reach into my pocket and pull out the nipple clamps I brought from her home. She doesn't even question anymore when I reveal something else I took from there. I lean forward licking and biting each of her nipples, alternating from one to the other until I'm satisfied with the peaks I've enticed for applying the clamps. "Hold out your wrist, Kitten, let me adorn you with bracelets." I lick and graze her neck with my teeth while slipping each leather cuff over her wrists. I lay my kitten down on her back and complete the frog tie bondage over each thigh and ankle, locking her in place.

"I could look at you like this for an eternity, Kitten," I run my hands up and down her inner thighs as I coo and praise her. "You look incredible laid out for me." I take a slow lick of her delicious center between each phrase. "Content to be used by me, pleasured by me, controlled by me, cherished by me, owned by me." I lean forward and kiss her mouth at the same time I gently remove her tail from her ass. I rub my finger over her asshole softly and dip inside, using my thumb to press on her clit. Her breath quickens, and she gasps and mews along with my touch.

"I made you something special, Kitty." I pull away briefly to apply fresh lubricant to her ass with my fingers. "Every pretty kitten needs a very special tail. One that fits perfectly. A tail that will keep her mind on her owner at all times." I hold the new tail into her view. It's the same color as her first. The fur is bushier, but still black with a white tip. The real difference is the plug, or well, lack of a plug. Instead, it's been fitted with a clone of my cock.

Slick rubber modeled veins and bulge with the beginning curve of my balls flared at the end. I bring it to her face and her mouth opens reflexively to ready welcome the cock. I oblige her with a few slow deep thrusts that earn me more moans and writhing of her body. After I pull it free of her lips, I rub it over her clit a few times before slathering it with lubricant.

I press the head of the cock up to her ass and apply gentle pressure until her body responds, relaxing her asshole to welcome my cock inside. Pulling it back and forth slowly, leisurely, working it farther and deeper. The view of watching my cock stretch and dive deep inside of her makes my actual cock ache for his turn. He'll have to wait though. I bend down to put my face to her pussy and absolutely devour her while keeping a steady pace with the tail. She bucks and jerks against the restraints, trying to find stability as I feast on her. She soaks my chin and her cum drips down my fingers that are wrapped around the tail cock, increasing the slip and slide of the dildo in her ass.

As she jerks and cries, I know what she's waiting for and it's killing her. "Cum pet, cum for your owner, your Sir. Cum for me, give me everything." My face buries into her, letting my stubble scrub against her as I double my pressure and the speed of the cock. She explodes. Screaming out her pleasure, body convulsing, incoherent moaning and whining. I shove the cock deep into her ass and I have my own cock thrusting into her melting hot pussy in a millisecond. Pressing my chest into hers, pulling on the chain of the nipple clamp. She whines and grunts, squeezing her pussy and jerking against her restraints. I wrap one arm behind her head and the other around her shoulder and press her to me. Her pussy squeezes me, and I can feel to the bulge of the cock in her ass with every thrust, the brush of the fur from her tail across my balls.

"You feel that, Kitten? That's me filling you up, only me. I will fill up every hole you have, in your body, and in your soul." I punctuate my words with my thrusts like I can bury them deep inside of her. "I complete you; I own you; I love you. And I WILL. NEVER. EVER. STOP." I fit my lips over hers and grunt my release into her mouth. I wrap my arms tighter around her and bury my face into her neck panting, like a wild man.

Kitty is quiet and still. Her body mush from the intense sex. After a few minutes of lying there together in silence, I slowly lean up and pull out of her. She has her eyes closed and her lashes are wet with a few tear streaks going down the sides of her face. "Did I hurt you, Kitten?" She shakes her head vigorously in a no. Relief. "Let me get you all cleaned up." I ease the cock from her ass, remove the frog ties, and the nipple clamps, rubbing her breast to massage away any discomfort. After I've bathed her and gotten her some water, I wrap her in a fluffy blanket and tuck her into bed. "I'll bring up some dinner and we can lay here together for the rest of the evening. How's that sound, Kitten?" Again, no words, she smiles softly and shakes her head in a little yes. I guess she is still coming down. I hurry to get her some food so I can get back and hold her.

In the kitchen, I grab a tray and load it up with cheese slices, fruit, and some slices of meat. My pet loves charcuterie-style munchies. I get a bottle of water and mix in a hydration multiplier as well. We were both covered in sweat afterward so I'm sure she could use it. I brace my hands on the countertop and take just a moment to breathe and get my mind straight.

I told her I loved her. I'm not surprised I said it, nor regretful, but I hadn't intended to tell her in that way. It came out in the passion. I won't take it back and I don't care if she doesn't feel the same yet. I assumed when I learned about Gary that it would take time for her to allow herself to trust someone else with her heart like that. I can wait. I still get to enjoy loving her in the meantime. I pick up the tray and the water and head back upstairs. When I get there, my pet has rolled over and fallen asleep. I set the water next to her on the nightstand and kiss the top of her head whispering, "You're such a good girl."

I head back downstairs and clean up the tray of food. Taking a beer from the refrigerator, I head out to the back patio and sit in one of the chairs by the firepit. I don't have the desire to light it, sitting under the solar patio lights is enough tonight. I scrub a hand over my face and sigh, I've always had a plan. A direct path. I deal in facts. Cold hard data. It is what it is and you can't argue with it. Sure, the people who come to me for my services come out of an abundance of emotion: rage, betrayal, fear, devastation... seeking revenge for whatever wrong they seem to have suffered. But what I give them is facts. Sure things, tangibility that they can move forward on. Being wrapped in emotion now feels foreign to me. Making every decision because I'm obsessed with the woman I saw in a laptop camera in the middle of a pawn shop.

Downing the beer and heading back inside, I lock up everything as I go, turning out lights and straightening blankets and pillows. I smile to myself with each one, thinking of my kitten lounging around in all her cozy places. We need to talk about the future. We can't put it off any longer; she has to go back to her shop and her friends. I head up the stairs to the bedroom, where she's still breathing softly, lying on her side facing away from the door. I strip off my t-shirt and slip under the covers next to her, throwing my arm and leg over her body. I rest my face behind her head and whisper in her ear. "I meant everything I have ever said to you, Kitten. You are a good girl. And you are mine. I will keep you." I fall asleep holding her, feeling at peace with her next to me. It's the deepest sleep I can ever remember. A stark contrast to the panic I feel when I wake up.

I sit up with a jolt, startled so hard from my deep sleep it physically hurts. The alarm is blaring downstairs. "Stay here, Kitten, go lock yourself in the bathroom!" I jump out of bed. I keep a small handgun safe mounted on the backside of the nightstand. I use my fingerprints to pop the lock and grab the gun. Heading toward the hall, I lock and close the bedroom door behind me. I creep down the stairs listening for any signs of activity. It's pitch black and silent. Even the solar patio lights have gone out. The stars and the moon send a few beams through the large windows that help me discern between shadows. We are far enough out here that there shouldn't be anyone accidentally happening upon the cabin. This alarm means the front door was opened. I take the bottom step and come into the main living area just in time to catch a flash of what looks like headlights leaving.

I want to race out after them, but I won't leave Kitten in the house alone. I turn off the alarm and turn on lights going room by room checking...nothing. There's no damage to the door frame. I pull up my security feed on my phone and head back upstairs to check on Kitty. It takes me a minute to get the bedroom door unlocked and I head to the bathroom where she should be waiting for me. Only, it's dark and empty. "Kitty! When I give you a directive that involves your safety, I *absolutely* expect it to be followed." I rip the covers back from where she is laying to find pillows instead of my woman. Shit!

Shit! "Kitten!" Shit. Shit. Shit. "KITTEN!!" I'm throwing bedding everywhere digging through blankets like I'm going to find her at the bottom. I look under the bed, the closet, the shower, and race up the hall to the spare room. "JOLIE!!!" Nothing. Silence. My phone is lying on the floor next to the bed. Quickly pulling up the security footage I confirm what the bile rising from my gut already tells me. It was her leaving that set off the alarm. Not an intruder. I watch and rewind, and watch again and again and again and again and again her walking right out the front door. She turns at the last second and looks back toward the stairs. Then she is gone. The feed from the front of the property shows her getting in her car and driving away. "FUCK!!!!!" I scream at the top of my lungs, hands on my head. I double over feeling like I'm gonna vomit.

I fucked up. I pushed too hard, too fast. I knew she wasn't ready before I started all this sweepstakes nonsense. But she was so sad without me. She needed me closer. I couldn't just take her to dinner like a nice guy would. No, I had to create an elaborate scheme and isolate her from her friends. FUCK! I slam my fist on the dresser and then pace back and forth. What can I do? If I go after her, I am going to scare the shit out of her and then there's no chance to ever get her back. I look around the room; she didn't take anything with her. Not her hairbrush, not her toothbrush, not her camera. She just left right from the bed.

In the security feed, she's wearing the little cotton kitty paja-ma set I gave her. I had dressed her in those tonight because I thought she needed something soft and comfortable. I crawl over the mountain I made out of bedding and lay with my face pressed straight into the mattress. My chest is on fire as I hold my breath, trying to calm the intense pain I feel at her absence. I finally take in a deep breath, getting her scent from the sheets. I need to think. I need to plan. I run my hand under the pillow intending to press it straight into my face, but my hand hits something crinkly. I sit up and find a piece of paper tucked under my pillow. The pretty script lettering of her handwriting is smeared with watermarks from fallen tears.

Dear Sir,

    I understand the cliché of saying this, but writing this letter really is the hardest thing I've ever done. Harder than signing my divorce papers, harder than explaining to my family that my marriage failed, and I was moving away, harder than starting over in a new town with nothing but a dream. I came to this cabin intending to find solitude to get over you. I started these 3 weeks feeling overwhelmed by how emotionally attached I am to you. Instead, I found myself pulled even deeper into your tide. This experience has been the MOST intense experience of my life. You consume me in all ways. It's terrifying. I know what I became after my ex-husband left. It will be nothing compared to the devastation I will feel if you decide to leave too. I'm a coward. I want to protect myself from that eventual heartache. How can this work in the real world? It's one thing to be living in the protective bubble of this cabin where there is nothing but the two of us, how can we work out there, where real life happens? And when you are bored of me, I will want to die from the grief. So, I am leaving now, while there still might be a chance for me to move on with dignity.

Yours,

Kitten

Oh, Kitten, you think you've left but I will always find you. I said I was going to keep you, and I meant it.

Chapter 16

Stray

Jolie

I BLINK AND SWIPE at my eyes. The tears that won't stop make it even harder to see in the dark on the road out here. There are no streetlights or anything to help with visibility for miles. His words echo on repeat in my mind. *"I complete you; I own you; I love you. And I WILL. NEVER. EVER. STOP."* It hurts so much already, knowing it's a lie. This is the kind of memory that burns itself into your brain. One that becomes so embedded that all your other thoughts grow around it. When the inevitable comes and he's done with me...this will be the memory that haunts my life. That follows me around every day, sits on my shoulder and whispers to me that I wasn't enough, wasn't worthy.

I can't continue under the lie, using every action or word from him to prop it up in my heart until I feel grounded and secure in that love, just to have it ripped away from me later. No, I'm making the right choice. I knew what I needed to do when I left for the cabin at the beginning of all this. I should have stuck to it. I should have left that first night and spent three weeks in solitude at home purging him from my chest. I swerve the car and slam the brakes, almost ending up in the ditch as a raccoon waddles across the road.

I need to get a grip on myself and get home safely, then I can go to pieces in privacy.

When I finally pull up to my house, the dark emptiness echoes the feeling in my insides. BB is with Krista, so I don't even have the sounds of her nails on the hallway or her little guffs to take the edge off. I don't have any bags to bring in because I left everything there. When Sir went downstairs to make food, I grabbed a notebook from my bag and hurriedly wrote him a goodbye letter. In my haste, I know I didn't adequately express myself and the strong emotions and doubts I'm having. I hope he understands what I was trying to convey. My bare feet are cold on the sidewalk and steps as I make my way up the porch and through my front door. Lost in thought, I remember faking being asleep and then slowly adding pillows between us so I could slip out of bed unnoticed, buying myself enough time to get my keys and make it out the front door.

I drop my keys three times trying to unlock my own front door. I wish BB was on the other side. I'm sobbing and my hands are shaking as I finally get the door unlocked. I lock myself in and then head straight to the kitchen. I pour myself a glass of water but can't bring myself to drink. What's the point? I should just waste away, there is no happiness without him. I turn toward the kitchen island bracing my hands on the countertop. Looking down, I see the sweepstakes letter. Rereading it now, I see so many clues. The website "secret mountain hideout," nontransferable...he was making sure I wouldn't bring or send Krista or Willow. I crumple the letter in my hands and in a sudden rage, I shred it up.

How dare he, HOW DARE HE!!! How dare he show me devotion, obsession, kindness...love? Look what he's done to me. I sink to the floor, leaning my back against the cabinets and pulling my knees in close. It's beginning to rain outside. The sounds of water hitting the roof and running down my windows play the soundtrack to my life. How do I go from Jolie-kitten submissive back to just Jolie? Jolie with no owner, Jolie with no Sir, Jolie with no love. I look down at the floor where a piece of the shredded letter had fallen. It's the last sentence from the body of the letter, "We just know you'll fall in love." I play with the piece of paper for a minute.

Standing up and I drag myself to my bedroom. I should shower but I'm not ready to wash his smell away just yet. The laptop is still on my dresser where I left it, but it is closed. I lay the scrap of letter on top of it and then crawl into bed. Thinking about the times he sent me groceries and changed my bedsheets, folded my clothes. He tried to take care of me in all ways. I'll never have the luxury again. The clock shows that it's almost dawn. I cry myself to sleep.

When I finally wake up it's late afternoon. I feel like shit, like I've been on an all-night bender. I get dressed and head to Krista's house. I need BB. She takes one look at me and turns nuclear. I don't have the energy to fight. So, I don't; instead, I fall on her couch and spill my guts. She is flabbergasted, to say the least. I sobbingly vomit out all the dirty details and my crazy mix of emotions until I'm hyperventilating with emotional panic.

"Okay, okay calm down. Jolie, you need to breathe." She hands me a glass with four fingers of whiskey because she said this wasn't a wine conversation. "Let me get this straight, you consented to all of these things, right?" I nod my head vigorously as I take a big sip. "Yes, absolutely; well I mean, I guess I didn't really consent to the stalking at first because I didn't know about it. Honestly, I don't care and think it was sweet." I take a smaller sip from my glass letting the burn spread through me. It reminds me of the taste of his mouth and then I'm fighting a new wave of tears.

"Uh, okay. I guess I can see that. He didn't try to hurt you. And he took down Gary, and he sent you and BB groceries…" We sit in silence for a few beats and then she speaks again. "Jolie, do you love him back?" I freeze, trying to find the breath to respond because I know when I open my mouth, I'll barely get the words out. I can't get it together enough, so I just vigorously nod my head. I lift my shaky hand and take another sip of whiskey. BB has her head in my lap and is looking up at me with her quiet, concerned eyes.

"Okay, okay, you love him, and he loves you. And you have a relationship dynamic that, while some would find unorthodox, you both find fulfilling." Krista looks at me for confirmation, so I just keep nodding my head. "Jolie, I would never judge you. I want you to find happiness and have your needs met. Whether that is in a relationship or not. The important thing is that you are happy, and you feel loved, and you know your worth." She rubs my shoulder soothingly. "I left him Krista! Now I'm just some sad stray woman who is never gonna know that kind of love again." I start another round of racking sobs.

"Do you want to stay here with me for a while? You and BB can hang out and I'll take care of the shop for a few more days to give you some time to process and get your bearings. You can stay as long as you want; hell, you can move in if you want." I sigh. I know she cares about me. I'm so grateful that I can talk to her without judgment. "No, I'm gonna take BB home. But I might take you up on the offer of watching the shop for a few more days though.

I need some time to get my shit together." She rubs my back and then leans her head to my shoulder. "Take all the time you need, babe, I'm here for you. You know that."

I've been torturing myself. I left my laptop on the dresser in the same place as before, but it sits closed now. I don't dare open it in case he is still watching. I want him to still be watching. I shouldn't want him to still be watching. I haven't been out of bed in three days. I shower and make sure BB's food and water bowls are full, then come straight back to bed. BB lays next to me. I hold the scrap of the letter in my hand and dwell in the past, in my memories of being a kitten with Sir. I'm snuggling with BB and a blanket. I press the fabric to my face, trying to suffocate the sadness out of me.

When I left the cabin without packing, I left my favorite blanket there too. Among other things that I had packed, and that Sir had confiscated from my home and packed for me. I've spent these days wearing the cute kitten pajamas he gave me and my ears. I'm so close to opening the laptop. I need to resist though. He stalked me; he interfered in my life. Did he brainwash me? Maybe he did that too because being without him feels so wrong. Like a part of myself is missing. I bury my face in BB's neck, she whines and pats me with her paw.

After a good hard cry, I lay in silence. BB is sleeping next to me. It's late, after midnight. I should be asleep too, but the lack of routine and daily activity has my day and night orientation all mixed up. Something outside snaps and BB is up in a flash, growling in warning. I try to pet her reassuringly and listen for more clues as to what that could have been. I locked all the doors, so I know we are safe. Maybe it's a possum. I hear it again, now it sounds like it's coming from my laundry room.

I slowly leave the bed, trying my best to be quiet. The door that separates the laundry room from the rest of the house on the inside is slightly ajar and vibrates with the sound of the next crack. I reach my hand out and move the door open just enough to see into the room. There is an arm reaching through the dog door and trying to unlock the doorknob. His fingers don't quite reach, the arm disappears and the cracking sound from before continues as he slams his body into the door trying to break it open. This time it works. Scott is standing in my doorway. BB growls and barks; she's put herself between Scott and me, my brave little baby.

"Well, hey there Jolie baby, say I really like those sweet little kitty cat ears you're wearing."

"You're supposed to be in, in *jail*."

"Yet here I am. I told you there would be consequences."

I slam the door and run for the bedroom. BB is right with me. I lock the door and look around frantically trying to figure out what to do next. I left my cell phone on the kitchen counter to charge. Stupid! I should have grabbed it on my way here. He's banging on the bedroom door. I slide my vanity table over to try to block it. It's the biggest piece of furniture here that I can move by myself. BB is going crazy. We are trapped here. It's only a matter of time before he comes through that door, I need to think. A weapon! What can I use as a weapon? Grabbing books off my bookshelf and I make them into a pile of projectiles. Think, think...I have a pair of scissors in my bathroom. Then I remember the laptop. Racing over to the dresser, I open the screen. My hands are shaking and the thump of Scott trying to break down the door is overpowering my thoughts.

The little red light glows by the camera. I peer straight in. "Sir, I don't know if you're there. Please be there. Scott is here. He's in the house trying to break down the door. Me and BB are locked in my bedroom. I need help, Sir, please, please be there."

BB is barking at the bedroom door, there is a particularly louder bang. When I look over, I fully expect Scott to have broken through. He hasn't but the wood is splintering, it won't be much longer. No matter what happens to me, I hope BB will be okay. I hope she runs away and finds a new home that loves her. She's so brave though, I know she won't leave my side. I can't bear the thought of Scott hurting her because she is protecting me. Something on the computer screen catches my eye and draws my attention back. The mouse is moving around, and the Word application is opening. Words begin to type on the screen.

Don't worry, Kitten. I'll always be here for you. I've already contacted 911 and officers have been dispatched to you. Push your bedside table into the bathroom. You and BB barricade yourselves in there. Everything is going to be okay. Trust me.

That's a good idea. I call BB as I swipe everything off the top of my nightstand and push it into the adjoining bathroom, close the door, and shove the nightstand against it. I dig through the drawers and find my scissors. I feel brave again. I'm channeling my inner tiger. I will fight for BB; I'll fight for myself. And I'm not alone, Sir is here with me. I just need to hold Scott off until the police arrive. I can do this. I hear the sharp splintering sound of the bedroom door breaking followed by the vanity table being knocked over. He's here.

"JJJJOooooLLLLIIIieeee" he sings my name. "Oh Jolie, there's my laptop. I should have known Frank would have sold it at the first opportunity, but I needed to stash it for a bit and I thought hiding it in plain site might work. Guess I was wrong." He slams a hand on the bathroom door to startle me.

"I'll admit, I'm surprised you were able to find the encrypted files though. I didn't peg you for having crazy computer skills. I guess we both misjudged each other. I thought you were just some dumb bitch running a hippie shop and you thought I was just gonna roll over and let you send me to jail." He slams his hand on the bathroom door again. I know he is toying with me. Good, let him take his time, the police are on their way, Sir said so. I try to remain quiet and calm. I don't want to spur him on with any heated words. BB is growling menacingly. He continues ranting about me and his crimes; why do villains always need to make big speeches right before they do more bad shit?

He starts putting his shoulder into the door and I raise my scissors ready to take this mother fucker out and protect myself and BB. I'm not going down without a fight. He is about to break all the way through; I can hear yelling from farther in the house. Hopefully, the police are here now. The wood of the bathroom door splinters and cracks as Scott breaks the door away from the frame, the nightstand blocks his entrance but there is a big enough opening to work his hand in, searching for the lock. I spring forward and jab him with my scissors hard enough to draw blood from his hand. Scott doesn't stop though; he continues to beat his way into the door, splinters falling, the nightstand scooting forward. I put my hands on it to try and hold it in place.

Looking up through the opening I watch as Scott gets pulled backward with a force followed by wet thumping sounds. BB jumps for the door and begins pawing, barking, and snarling. I try to hold her back, but she is determined to get in on the action on the other side of the door. I hear the bark of an authoritative male voice and freeze. It isn't the police; it's Sir, and Sir is **pissed**.

"Fuck you Peterman, I allowed you to keep your arms once after touching what's mine but this time there'll be no holding back!" I peer through the splintered crack in the door to see Sir waylaying Scott. Scott lays on the floor beneath him, Sir holding him up by the collar and striking him with his fist straight to the face. Scott's face is a bloody mess and struggling does nothing to help him escape Sir's firm grasp. BB continues to go nuts trying to get out there and help. "What were you gonna do, Peterman? Break in here and take your own bad decisions out on a woman? You and Congressman Roberts are finished." Sir picks Scott up by the front of his shirt with both hands and growls into his face... "I will spend every second of the rest of my life making sure you never get parole, you get all the shitty work details, and you get housed in the worst possible prison for your crimes. If you so much as shit in the wrong toilet, I'll know, and I'll make sure you suffer."

I see the flash of blue and red coming through the bedroom window. The police have finally arrived. Thankfully Sir got here because if I had really had to wait on the police, I'm sure I would be a goner at this moment. I'm clutching the scissors in the center of my chest as I watch the police rush into my bedroom and take Scott out of Sir's hands. The sheriff and Sir shake hands and the police drag Scott away. I haven't moved from my view here in the bathroom, I haven't breathed. I don't know what to do. I can't make my body do anything. BB is sitting patiently next to my feet, her tail thumping against my ankles is the only sensation I register.

"Kitten, can you move the nightstand so I can come in?" Sir's voice is soft, placating. He is looking back at me through the crack in the door. I blink a few times to try to make my brain work but I can't. All I can do is stare back at him. "Hey little kitty, it's time to come out from there." He tries again. This time I can exhale and I shakily move my hands from my chest to the nightstand and give it a push to let the door come part way open. Sir slips through, coming into the bathroom with me. He sits on the rug and holds his arms out to me. Bursting into a fit of sobs, I melt into his lap. So grateful for the arms that are here to hold me and the eyes that have watched over me. He rubs my back in soothing circles whispering praises into my hair. "What a good girl, a brave girl. You did good, Kitty, you did really good."

CHAPTER 17
FOREVER

Sir

THE LEATHER OF THE car seat groans underneath me as I adjust my position. I've been sitting in this car for hours and my back and neck feel stiff. I'm honestly surprised no one has called the cops to report a suspicious vehicle parked in the neighborhood. I couldn't stay at the cabin knowing she was here and upset. I tracked her cell phone until I knew she made it to her house, never taking my eyes off the little red dot traveling her route home. Then I watched through cameras I had installed as she fell to pieces. It killed me that I wasn't there to put her back together. The keys were in my hand before I could even think through what my plan was.

She needs some space, and some time to understand what we really mean to each other. I know she'll come around. And the second she does I will be there to scoop her up. That's why I need to be close. Until then, I'll watch every move she makes. She leaves the laptop closed, thinking that's keeping me out. I tracked her phone to Krista's house and back when she went to pick up BB. I watched her every second of the day and night while she wasted in sadness the following days. All I can do is sit in my car parked a few streets over in her neighborhood, waiting, and working; until Congressman Roberts is also arrested, Peterman could still pose a threat. Lawrence is helping me keep watch on Peterman until I am sure he is completely out of the picture.

I scrub my hand over my face as I watch her scream into her blanket. If she would leave the house, I would slip in and return all her belongings. I hate that she doesn't have her special blanket to hold right now. My phone vibrates with a call. I switch it to speaker and don't take my eyes off Kitten. Lawrence's panicked voice fills my car. "Peterman is gone." What the fuck. He has my attention now. "What do you mean gone?" I can hear the clicking of a keyboard in the background. "I mean I can't find him on any of the cameras. The facial recognition in the jail can't find him. All his records are wiped."

Fuck. My brain is working through the possibilities, then the camera I have for her backyard gets movement. "Lawrence, get the cops out here now!" I throw the car in gear and squeal my tires as I drive to her home nearly taking out a few mailboxes. As I turn the corner, I get an alert on my phone that the laptop is open. Kitten is pleading through the screen for me to help her. I quickly send her a message and then I'm out of the car like lightning. As I race up the front porch, I have the key ready and it feels like an eternity to unlock this door. Screaming her name through the living room and kitchen, I make my way to the bedroom where she said she was hiding. The house is in complete disarray where Peterman overturned anything that wasn't nailed down to strike fear into her.

The bedroom is even worse. There are broken pieces of wood all over the floor. The bedroom door is hanging by a single hinge, and makeup and hair products are scattered everywhere. Her vanity is lying on its side partly blocking the entrance. Peterman is busting down the bathroom door, yelling obscenities at my kitten. My world turns red, then I lose myself to the emotion and utterly fuck him up for coming anywhere near her. Before he even registers that I'm in the room with him, I have his shirt in my hand, and I jerk him backward and to the ground. I slam my fist into him over and over. Blood from his nose spurts upward as I crack the bone. I want to hit him so hard that he gets amnesia and forgets her face and why he's here.

I'm screaming threats in his face when the police finally arrive. Blue and red lights flash from the street. The officers have guns drawn; I drop Peterman and lift my hands, backing away from him. He sputters and gasps from the floor. Peterman launches into a fabrication that I attacked him for no reason, and he wants to press assault charges. The officer lifts Peterman from the floor, cuffing him, and begins reading him his rights. Peterman jerks his body in an attempt to resist but trips over a pile of books in the middle of the floor and falls to his knees. Another officer joins the first and they haul Peterman out of the house.

The sheriff approaches me and reaches to shake my hand. "No, worries about Peterman, he's going right back to jail. We have the still images from your home security footage showing him breaking down the door and threatening your wife. She can come down to the station in a few days and give her statement. Do either of you need medical care?" Lawrence is getting a raise. I don't correct the sheriff about mine and Kitty's relationship, but I file the "wife" idea away for later, when she's ready.

"No sheriff, thankfully we are fine. Let me know if you need any more evidence from the security cameras." I take a deep breath as he leaves. The adrenaline is coming down now, I look around at the carnage of her bedroom. Books are strowed over the floor, her makeup crushed and staining the carpet, the vanity is busted. Wooden splinters are littered by the bedroom and bathroom doors. Thank God I was close by, or he would have been through that bathroom door in seconds. I can't allow myself to think about what might have happened.

Kitten, she's standing on the other side of the bathroom door peering through the splintered opening in the wood. Her sweet face contradicts the chaos of broken doors and turned-over furniture that liters her bedroom. Her little sanctuary desecrated by that scum. She's still holding her scissors. The imagery of her fighting for her life with Peterman with only a pair of sewing scissors makes my gut turn. The tips are stained red with blood, and more is smeared in the center of her little cat pajamas. Everything that has led to me standing here on the other side of her door plays through my mind like a movie trailer.

The first moment I saw her face, all those nights in her bathtub, watching her sleep, following her around town. Learning everything I could about her interests, her desires. Teaching her how to find herself as a submissive. Watching her blossom under my training into the perfect pet. A kitten after my own heart. We didn't come this far to walk away. I won't let her walk away from everything we have.

"Kitten, can you move the nightstand so I can come in?" She doesn't move, I'm not even sure she registered that I'm speaking to her. She blinks a few times but that's it. I soften my voice, "Hey little kitty, it's time to come out from there." This time the fog seems to lift a little and she scoots the nightstand a few inches out of the way. Good, this is progress. She could've told me to get the fuck out. I slip into the bathroom and sit on the rug, holding my hands out to her. She slips to the floor. I take the scissors out of her hand and set them aside. Sitting on the floor with her in my lap I finally feel whole again.

The tension in my chest starts to ease as I rub her back and whisper in her ear. This is what I was made for. Taking care of my Kitten. We stay like this as the police move around her home taking pictures. We stay like this after they leave, and the sun starts to rise. Lawrence has been sending me updates by text; I can depend on him to take over with Peterman so I can focus on her.

I pet her back and her hair; subconsciously I had started to hum the melody to "Give" by Sleep Token. "Do you know the words to that song?" she asks. It was so quiet I almost didn't hear her. "Yes, I do Kitten." I sing to her softly while her head rests against my shoulder. Whisper singing these lyrics to her in the context of everything that has happened, I feel them in a way I hadn't before...I hope she hears it too. BB licks my hand and nudges my elbow looking for her turn for a pet. This dog. I've grown quite fond of her in my visits to Kitty's home. Reaching over I scratch her head to thank her for trying to protect our girl until I could get here.

Tears begin on my shoulder again, so I tighten my hold on her. "I'm so sorry, I just freaked out. I shouldn't have left like that. I did the exact thing that I was scared would happen to me." She buries her face deeper into me. Squeezing me back. "Kitten, there's nowhere you can go that I won't follow, I'll find you anywhere and bring you back to where you belong, with me." I rise from the floor, scooping her up to carry her over the broken pieces of wood on the bedroom floor. We head down the porch, where I buckle her in my car and open the back door for BB. She doesn't say anything, doesn't ask questions. She just trusts me to lead her.

I take her and BB back to the cabin. My kitten needs some care. I put her in the shower and give her a good hard scrub from head to toe. I know she loves hot water and rough scrubbing to cope with stress. Her wet hair is a mess sticking to her face and neck. I take my time putting in the conditioner and gently combing out the tangles. Once she's dressed in fresh pajamas and her collar is on, I put her to bed to rest. Hearing that little bell jingle again was balm to my soul. BB is lounging next to me on the couch while I follow up with Lawrence about what happened.

Congressman Roberts used his witness protection contact to extract Peterman from jail. They thought if they got the laptop back, they could destroy the origin of the evidence against them thinking it would help them refute its validity. Lawrence posed as an FBI agent with Homeland Security and presented the evidence he found that identified the Congressman's witness protection contact; he has also been arrested.

I contacted Krista and filled her in on everything that has happened. After she felt assured that her friend was truly safe, I got my ass chewed about treating her well and never breaking her heart. I'm glad my pet has such loyal friends; I hope to never end up on Krista's bad side. I sent Davis over to sit at the shop with Krista for a few days. She could use an extra hand after working on her own for these past few weeks and I feel better knowing Krista isn't there alone until the dust settles with the congressman and Peterman. Once those ends are tied, BB and I head upstairs.

I climb into bed behind Kitten and pull her close to me, inhaling the smell of her skin and hair. I never imagined how taking this job would have changed my life. It was just another case. But it brought me my kitten, my forever. For now, I'm going to sleep next to her warmth and enjoy the comfort of her next to me back in the secluded bubble of our mountain cabin. When we wake, I have some planning to do.

Falling back into our routine, I'm already downstairs working at the kitchen island when she makes her way down. The jingle of her collar precedes her. I might never let her take that thing off again, lest she forget her place with me. I pull out a barstool for her to sit, then get to work making her breakfast. I set a cup of lavender tea in front of her. Her face remains downcast with a sad expression. The clink of the spoon, while I dip her yogurt, is the only sound echoing in the kitchen. I set the bowl in front of her then sprinkle in some blueberries and drizzle honey over. She doesn't make a move toward the food, so I slide onto my own barstool and lift the spoon to her mouth. "Eat, Kitten." Dutifully she opens her mouth for me to pop the spoon in. Chewing slowly, she keeps her eyes focused on the countertop in front of her.

I didn't want to push her today, but it seems I'll need to. "If you don't speak to me Kitten, I can't make anything better." Her eyes water with tears she is fighting, and a little drool collects at the corners of her mouth as she tries to swallow her food before a sob can break free. With shaky words, she pours out her heart to me. "I was a bad girl. I let my feelings of inadequacy and fear of eventual rejection overwhelm me. I didn't trust you, or even give you the option of proving yourself."

Sobs rack her chest as she struggles to get the words out. I wait patiently for her finish but it's difficult not to reach out and scoop her up. She continues, "I let my fear blind me to all the things you've done. The care you showed me, the consistency in your actions, your affection...I am so sorry, I need to do something to make it right." She turns to face me now, eyes pleading. "Give me something I can do to make it right"

I exhale deeply, taking in what she's asking for. "Kitten, I won't punish you for having fears and doubts. You should have talked to me instead of leaving. Driving in the middle of the night down the mountain path was dangerous. But you aren't a prisoner here with me." I lift the teacup to her lips and urge her to take a drink. "I suppose this could fall under your rule about knowing your worth. My good pet should understand what she means to Sir and that I will do whatever is needed to prove that to you. Open communication between us is necessary and expected, Kitten."

I lift the spoon again to her mouth, feeding her another bite. "After you finish your breakfast, we will take care of this." She lets out a relieved sigh and allows me to continue feeding her breakfast and give her sips of tea. Once the dishes are taken care of, I leave her at the counter while I head toward the back door to the patio area. Her leash is on a hook next to the entryway there. I return and clip it to her collar then silently lead her upstairs. Her face full of trepidation, unsure of what I could possibly come up with as a consequence.

I pass up the bed and head into the bathroom, her face turns more uncertain. I figure she thought I'd tie her to the bed and spank her ass red and raw. I have a better idea though.

"It seems we need a little more training, pet." Looping the cuff of the leash over the towel rod, I pull a permanent marker from my back pocket. "You enjoy writing on yourself Kitty, but you're shit at picking out the right things to say about yourself. Always covering yourself in hurtful lies. I'm going to fix that. Instead of your eyeliner, I'm going to use this permanent marker and you will wear my words on your skin until they soak into your soul. If that isn't enough, next time I'll tattoo them on you. Now strip." I watch with my arms folded and pinning her with my best authoritative stare while she disrobes. I move to stand behind her, making a big show of uncapping the marker. I begin writing on her skin all the things I need her to remember. She watches on in the mirror as I transform her naked body into my own work of art.

Across her chest, I write: *This kitten belongs to Sir, always and in all ways.* Down her breast, ribs, and belly:

Sir's nipples. Lush bounty.

Beautiful.

Loved. Adored. Owned.

Your place is with Sir.

Worthy.

I correct every ugly thing I've ever witnessed her write on herself and then some. I lift her leg up and to the side so I can write on her inner thighs. *Delicious. Exquisite. Succulent, Heavenly. Sir's pussy.* I continue until she is covered in my words from her neck to her knees. "You can wear your robe today, but no other clothes. I won't let you cover up my words until you've learned your lesson,

Kitten." The rest of the day is spent with physical connection, no sex because this isn't about sex. This is about the us that transcends the desires of the flesh. Lounging on the porch swing bed, she lays her head in my lap while I caress her breast under the fabric of her rob and read to her. The gentle sway of the swing and the sounds of nature bring peace after so much challenge. BB frolics in the front yard trying to catch a lizard that's playing hard to get.

"I love you too, Sir." I immediately stopped swinging. My hand freezes on her breast. She continues, "I have known my deep feelings for you for a long time. And I've been running from them ever since. It's why I accepted the sweepstakes prize in the first place." Kitten sits up to face me, placing her hand against my jaw and peering into my eyes, hers full of emotion. "I needed your relentless pursuit, I need your control, I need you." Tears trickle over her cheeks. I press my lips to hers and pull her into my lap. Whispering back to her without letting my lips leave hers I say, "And you will always have me, Kitten."

Epilogue

Sir

Mildew fills my nostrils as I make my way down the dimly lit hallway. The fluorescent light reflects off the vomit-yellow of the walls and floor creating an ominous atmosphere, perfect for the task at hand. The dissonant creak of the heavy metal door signals my arrival as I enter the interview room. Seated and handcuffed to the metal table is a very confused Jonah Peterman.

"Who the fuck is this? You're not my lawyer!" Peterman's face contorts with contempt as he eyes me up and down. I lean against the wall in the far corner and tip my chin at the guard who returns my nod and exits the room. It's just the two of us now. "Looks like you've been having a rough time in here Peckerman," I say. "Someone been using you as a punching bag lately?" I push off the cold cinderblock wall and take a few steps closer to the table, keeping my hands concealed in my pockets.

"It's Peterman, and who the fuck are you? Where's my regular guy?" His speech is slightly off due to his busted lip and missing front teeth. I can't help the smile that spreads across my face. "You don't recognize me?" I lean a little closer bringing my face out of the shadow. Peterman narrows his brows as he takes me in. "I'm the guy that beat the shit out of for breaking into my woman's house."

It's a fucking chore to keep my posture relaxed and my voice calm as the memories of what I walked into that night come back.

His shoulders tense, the only sign of recognition as he too tries to maintain a façade of cool confidence. "Why are you here?" His fists squeeze as he braces his hands against the cuffs, blanching the skin of his wrists and knuckles. Good, he should be scared. "You smell like shit. Haven't you been showering?" He doesn't respond. I smile because I know why. I know all the answers. I am all the answers. "Is it because you're getting jumped anytime you let your guard down in here? ...A beat down as you leave the mess hall...shank to the belly while walking the yard... waterboarded with piss while you try to take a shit?" I slowly stalk my way around the metal table, taking the long way around toward him, tapping the brass knuckles I'm wearing on the table top as I go. Ching. Ching. Ching.

"Where the fuck is the guard," he says through gritted teeth; well, as many teeth as he can grit. Peterman shifts nervously in his seat, his anxiety growing stronger. He jerks at the cuffs fruitlessly. "Guard! Hey Guard! Where the FUCK ARE YOU?! THIS SHITHEAD'S CRAZY, MAN!" He yells toward the door, but nothing happens.

"Hmmm, it's like they don't give a rat's ass what happens in here." I briefly pause my tapping to tip my head in fake contemplation. Sweat is beading on Peterman's brow and upper lip; his chest begins to heave. "They got cameras in here, dumbass. You'll never get away with this and then what? You'll be right here with me."

"They aren't recording anything right now." I watch with rapt satisfaction as the color drains from Peterman's face. He clears his throat and then asks, "How do you know they aren't recording?" His tone tries to convey some semblance of retained confidence. Clinging to any frayed edges of hope he has that I might be bluffing. I'm not. Pressing the edge of the brass knuckles into the metal table I scrape them down the length of it, sskkkkrrreeeee, the sharp sound offending even my ears. He jerks back in his chair again, but it doesn't budge. My prey is trapped. "I used to do favors for the mafia, Jonah, now they do favors for me. You see; when you took her to coffee, I thought a quick hit while you're in prison would be enough—but then you really fucked up — Now, I would never be satisfied unless I got my own hands dirty."

He tries to slide down into the chair, anything he can do to put more space between us. I nod my head as I speak, slow my pace to him, I want to draw out every ounce of fear I can. I want to bathe in it. I want to bottle it up so that when the memories of her cowering in her bathroom with BB come back to haunt me, I can take it out and savor the aroma of my retribution.

"It won't matter how loud you yell... It won't matter how much of a mess I make." I've made my way around the table now. I place my hand on his shoulder and squeeze it as I round behind him. "What was that you told her? ...That there would be consequences?" The smell of fresh piss permeates the air followed by a trickling sound as it runs down his leg to the concrete floor. I lean in close. "There are consequences —," I say. From behind I whisper in his ear. "Only one of us is leaving this room — and it's definitely NOT you."

In the following weeks, Kitten and I worked out some healthy boundaries in our relationship. She knows where all the cameras are that I placed in her home and shop, tracking her phone... She agreed to allow some of my stalking to stay in place out of safety. And it appears my kitten has some voyeur tendencies. There was a little hiccup when she realized the extent of my efforts on the dating website and that I was also Justin and every other account on the site. I just shrugged. What can I say, I'm obsessed. From the moment I saw her at the pawn shop I have had one singular purpose; her.

And it still is. I obtained the ownership of Peterman's outdoor business and revamped it to be my new home base. We front as an electronics repair shop. It's now my main point of business so I can be close to Kitten. We have lunch every day at the coffee shop with Krista, Willow, and Davis. Davis seems to have developed a close friendship with Krista after being at the shop with her while Kitten and I worked out our kinks, pun intended.

Congressman Roberts is en route for prison along with his accomplice in witness protection. The judicial system isn't dragging its feet with this one; that's largely due to the pressure being applied by his wife, her petition of the congressman's constituents, and the landslide of evidence my team has put together on him. Shortly after Peterman was sentenced, he was found dead in his cell. I guess he pissed off the wrong man.

Kitten and I decided to start over with a new home. Still small and cozy, but a place that belongs to us and isn't marred by the traumatic memories of Peterman's break-in and assault. We still have the cabin for when we need an escape, like this weekend for example.

My perfect little kitty waits on her hands and knees for me to apply her paw mittens. Her collar jingles happily as she wiggles with delight. She licks at my fingers while I pull the mittens over her hands. I lift a teacup of blueberries from the end table. "Does my little kitty want a treat?" She reaches up my thighs and paws at me in earnest. "You'll need to work for it, Kitty. Let's see...can Kitty sit on her hind paws?" She pops back, balancing in deep open squat, her knees wide giving me a mouth-watering view of her bare pussy, her front paws braced over the tops of her breasts. "Very good." I toss a blueberry in the air for her to catch in her mouth. She is shit at catching them, taking it to the face every time with a pout. It's adorable, I hope she never improves. I pick up a fresh one and pop it right into her mouth.

"What other tricks does my Kitty know? How about showing Sir your best stretch?" She turns her body away from me, so her ass is pointed in my direction, arching her back and lifting her ass into the air. She looks over her shoulder at me with a sly expression and wiggles her ass making her tail swish side to side. "Very nice Kitty, another blueberry for you." I set down the cup and thread my fingers into her hair while she munches down on her treat. Running one hand down to pinch and twist her nipple. Kitty moans in delight.

I guide her to lay on her back on the rug and have her use her front paws to hold her feet up and out for me. Kneeling behind her ass, I pick up her hips and roll them forward, lifting them up so I can bury my face in her wet pussy, the fur of her tail tickling my chin. I eat her out with delight, spurred by her mews. She's started meowing during sex and it makes me hard as fuck. I suck and nip at her clit, dipping my tongue into her and then licking upward over her pussy, trying to get every drop of juice she seeps. Keeping her hips lifted, I slide my knees underneath to support her and slip my pulsing hard cock into her swollen pussy. Holding her hips I grind into her, relishing in the softness of her tail caressing my balls and cum soaking my cock. I grind my pelvis into her clit until she meows and cums hard.

I slip my arms under her shoulders and press my body over hers, rutting into her like a wild man. I pull her hair to turn her head so my lips line up with her ear. I lick and bite her earlobe and her neck, living for every gasp and moan I wring from her. "My good girl. My dirty pet, I found you, I trained you, and I'll keep you always. Always. You're mine, Kitty, forever, you're mine."

The End

Acknowledgements

First, I would like to say…I initially had no intention of publishing this book. I have always loved to read and love the romance genre. The idea of writing my own started as a private pastime. After I finished the first draft of Chapter 1, I closed my laptop and reassured myself that this was no big deal and just something private and fun for me.

Then I shared what I was up to with some very close friends. It was their energy and enthusiasm that propelled me forward.

Thank you to my husband for giving me space to work on this project and for your supporting words.

Thank you to my brother who has championed every crazy idea I've ever had. Everyone needs someone in their life that always says "Yes, and damn the consequences", you are my person. Thank you also for saying you were proud of me. Your words helped me see something I was trying to keep small for as big and as important as it really was.

Thank you also to some very special friends. Thank you for all your help with self-editing and cheering me on as this story developed. Thank you for being the kind of friends I can trust with a project so dear to my heart.

To everyone who has encouraged me, thank you so much for being with me on this journey to try something new, create something fun, and take this from a concept to reality. I love you all so much.

About the Author

J.P. Newmon was born and raised in Louisiana. She is a lover of all forms of art and enjoys photography, drawing, painting, and multimedia work in addition to writing. Her debut novel, Training Sweet Jolie: Book 1 of the Dirty Voyeurs series, released in January of 2025, and she looks forward to many works to follow. Romance by JP is a unique blend of authentic emotional journey and shockingly spicy intimacy. Her love for reading and the romance genre is what inspired her to take the leap from reader to self-published author. When she isn't writing romance, she is kept busy being a mom and working full-time.

Need more JP Newmon?

Follow @JPNewmonauthor on various social media platforms

Visit her website https://jpnewmonauthor.com/and sign up for her newsletter to get updates and previews on upcoming projects.

Coming Later this Year

If you enjoyed Jolie and Sir's story then you may also want to check out my next installment in the Dirty Voyeurs series, *Dripping for Her Pleasure*, a spicy paranormal romance.

Dripping for Her Pleasure

Dirty Voyeurs Book 2

By

J. P. Newmon

Fredrick: My spirit has been trapped in an antique bottle for years by mysterious and supernatural forces; my existence feels bleak. Thinking I was doomed to an eternity of isolation, everything changed when she walked into my "life".

Willow: I've always loved the rare and unusual...drawn to the macabre. Now the supernatural world has come full force into my life, and it feels so so very ...right.